Ella Wheeler Wilcox

Shells

Ella Wheeler Wilcox

Shells

ISBN/EAN: 9783337389673

Printed in Europe, USA, Canada, Australia, Japan

Cover: Foto ©Andreas Hilbeck / pixelio.de

More available books at **www.hansebooks.com**

SHELLS.

BY

ELLA WHEELER.
Author of "Drops of Water" and other Poems.

MILWAUKEE:
HAUSER & STOREY.
1873.

DEDICATION.

PREFACE.

By the waves of thought, these "Shells" were washed out upon the shores of imagination, and I gathered them in idle moments. If they shall give you a few hours enjoyment, it will add to the pleasure I experienced in making the collection.

ELLA WHEELER.

CONTENTS

TO SECOND EDITION.

CONTENTS.

CONTENTS.

CONTENTS.

END.

SHELLS.

OUR LIVES.

Our lives are songs.   God writes the words,
  And we set them to music at pleasure ;
And the song grows glad, or sweet, or sad,
  As we choose to fashion the measure.

We must write the music, whatever the song,
  Whatever its rhyme, or metre ;
And if it is sad, we can make it glad,
  Or if sweet, we can make it sweeter.

One has a song that is free and strong ;
  But the music he writes is minor ;
And the sad, sad strain is replete with pain,
  And the singer becomes a repiner.

And he thinks God gave him a dirge-like lay,
  Nor knows that the words are cheery ;
And the song seems lonely and solemn—only
  Because the music is dreary.

And the song of another has through the words
    An under current of sadness ;
But he sets it to music of ringing chords,
    And makes it a pean of gladness.

So whether our songs are sad or not,
    We can give the world more pleasure,
And better ourselves, by setting the words
    To a glad, triumphant measure.

1872.

THE MESSENGER.

She rose up, in the early dawn,
    And white, and silently she moved
About the house :   Four men had gone
    To battle for the land they loved :
And she, the mother, and the wife,
Waited for tidings from the strife.
How still the house seemed ; and her tread
Sounded like footsteps of the dead.

The long day passed.   The dark night came.
    She had not seen a human face.
Some voice spoke suddenly her name.
    How loud it sounded in that place
Where, day on day, no sound was heard
But her own footsteps.   "Bring you word,"

She cried, to whom she could not see—
"Word from the battle plain to me?"
A soldier entered at the door,
   And stood within the dim firelight.

"I bring you tidings of the four"
   He said, "Who left you for the fight."
"God bless you friend!" she cried, "speak on!"
For I can bear it.   "One is gone?"
"Ay! one is gone!" he said, "Which one?"
"Dear lady—he, your eldest son."

A deathly pallor shot across
   Her withered face : she did not weep.
She said, "It is a grievous loss,
   But God gives his beloved sleep.
What of the living—of the three,
And when can they come back to me?"
The soldier turned away his head,
"Lady, your husband too, is dead."

She put her hand upon her brow.
   A wild, sharp pain, was in her eyes,
"My husband? oh God help me now."
   The soldier shivered at her sighs.
The task was harder than he thought.
"Your youngest son, dear madam, fought
Close at his father's side : both fell
Dead, by the bursting of a shell."

She moved her lips and seemed to moan.
   Her face had paled to ashen grey—
"Then one is left me—one alone,"
   She said, "of four who marched away.
Oh Over-ruling, All-wise God,
How can I pass beneath Thy rod!"
The soldier walked across the floor,
Paused at the window, at the door—

Wiped the cold dew drops from his cheek
   And sought the mourner's side again.
"Once more, dear lady, I must speak.
   Your last remaining son was slain
Just at the closing of the fight,
'Twas he who sent me here to-night."
"God knows," the man said afterward,
"The fight itself, was not as hard."

                    1871.

IDLE.

I sit in the twilight dim,
   At the close of an idle day,
And list to the sweet, soft hymn
   That rises far away
     And dies on the evening air.
Oh all day long they sing their song
   Who toil in the valley there.

But never a song sing I,
  Sitting with folded hands.
The hours pass me by,
  Dropping their golden sands.
    And I list from day to day
  To the tick, tick, tock, of the old brown clock
    Ticking my life away.

And I see the sunlight fade,
  And I see the night come on ;
And then, in the gloom and shade,
  I weep for the day that is gone.
    Weep, and wail, in pain,
  For the misspent day that has flown away
    And will not come again.

Another morning beams,
  But I forget the last,
And sit in my idle dreams
  Till the day is overpast.
    Oh the toiler's heart is glad
  When the day is gone and the night comes on,
    But mine is sore, and sad.

For I dare not look behind :
  No shining, golden sheaves
Can I ever hope to find—
  Nothing but withered leaves.

Ah ! dreams are very sweet !
But will it please if only these
    I lay at the Master's feet.

And what will the Master say,
    To dreams and nothing more ?
Oh idler all the day !
    Think, ere thy life is o'er !
        And when the day grows late,
    Oh soul of sin, will He let you in
        There at the pearly gate ?

Oh idle heart beware !
    On, to the field of strife!
On to the valley there,
    And live a useful life.
        Up ! do not wait a day,
    For the old brown clock, with its tick, tick, tock,
        Is ticking your life away.

                                        1869.

YE AGENTS.

These agent men ! these agent men !
We hear the dreaded step again,
We see a stranger at the door;
And brace ourselves for war once more.

He bows and smiles. "Walk in," we say,

He smiles again. " I come to-day,
Dear Madam, with a great invention ;
And Sir, pray give me *your* attention ;
Now here, you see, is something new,
And just the thing, my friends, for you."

In vain we interrupt and say :
" We shall not buy of you to-day."
"But, Madam, Sir, you have not seen
The beauties of this new machine ;
When thus arranged, your old affair,
'Tis plain to see, is just nowhere."
" No doubt," I say; "'Tis very fine,
And quite superior to mine."
This gives him courage. On he goes,
And every sentence glibly flows,
Until his lesson is repeated
To "warranted if fitly treated."

"Yes, new and fine, and grand," we say,
"But still we shall not buy to-day."
" But, Madam, Sir, pray list to reason,
'Twill buy itself in half a season ;
You see the thing is bound to go."
"Oh certainly, we see, we know,
But still we do not wish to buy."
He turns and leaves us with a sigh,

And while we hasten to our labor
He goes and persecutes our neighbor.

But lo ! another follows on,
Before the last is fairly gone.
One day a reaper, next a mower,
And then a fanning mill, and sower ;
Machines of all kinds 'neath the sun,
Each better than the other one ;
A rocker for each dining chair,
A brace to hold the broom in air,
A book, just out, and you must buy
Or give a proper reason why.

So if we sometimes turn away
Abruptly, Sirs, you must remember,
That we have heard your tale each day
From early Spring to late December.
Why ! if we listened to you all,
And gave you the required attention,
I think ere long each one would call,
The " county house," the *best* invention.

1869.

WARNED.

They stood at the garden gate.
By the lifting of a lid

She might have read her fate
   In a little thing he did.

He plucked a beautiful flower,
   Tore it away from its place
On the side of the blooming bower,
   And held it against his face.

Drank in its beauty and bloom,
   In the midst of his idle talk ,
Then cast it down to the gloom
   And dust of the garden walk.

Ay, trod it under his foot,
   As it lay in his pathway there ;
Then spurned it away with his boot,
   Because it had ceased to be fair.

Ah ! the maiden might have read
   The doom of her young life then ;
But she looked in his eyes instead,
   And thought him the king of men.

She looked in his eyes and blushed,
   She hid in his strong arms' fold ;
And the tale of the flower, crushed
   And spurned, was once more told.

2

LIFE.

An infant wailing in nameless fear ;
  A shadow, perchance, in the quiet room,
Or the hum of an insect flying near,
  Or the screech-owl's cry, in the outer gloom.

A little child on the sun-checked floor,
  A broken toy, and a tear stained face,
A young life clouded, a young heart sore ;
  And the great clock, time, ticks on apace.

A maiden weeping in bitter pain,
  Two white hands clasped on an aching brow.
A blighted faith and a fond hope slain,
  A shattered trust and a broken vow.

A matron holding a baby's shoe,
  The hot tears gather, and fall at will
On the knotted ribbon of white and blue,
  For the foot that wore it is cold and still.

An aged woman upon her bed,
  Worn, and wearied, and poor and old,
Longing to rest with the happy dead,
  And thus the story of life is told.

Where is the season of careless glee ?
   Where is the moment that holds no pain ?
Life has its crosses from infancy
   Down to the grave ; and its hopes are vain.

                  1870.

STARS.

Astronomers may gaze the heavens o'er,
   Discovering wonders, great, perhaps, and true !
That stars are worlds, and peopled like our own,
   But I shall never think as these men do.

I shall believe them little shining things,
   Fashioned from heavenly ore, and filled with light.
And to the sky above, so smoothly blue,
   An angel comes and nails them, every night.

And I have seen him.   You no doubt would think
   A white cloud, sailed across the heavens blue.
But as I watched the feathery thing, it was
   An angel nailing up the stars I knew.

And all night long they shine for us below ;
   Shine in pale splendor, till the mighty sun
Wakes up again.   And then the angel comes,
   And gathers in his treasures, one by one.

How sweet the task !   Oh when this life is done,
   And I have joined the angel band on high,
Of all that throng, oh may it be my lot,
   To nail the stars upon the evening sky.

                     1868.

FADING.

She sits beside the window.   All who pass
   Turn once again to gaze on her sweet face.
She is so fair ; but soon, too soon, alas,
   To lie down in her last low resting place.

No gems are brighter than her sparkling eyes.
   Her brow like polished marble, white and fair—
Her cheeks as glowing as the sunset skies—
   You would not dream that death was lurking there.

But, oh ! he lingers closely at her side,
   And when the forest dons its Autumn dress,
We know that he will claim her as his bride,
   And earth will number one fair spirit less.

She sees the meadow robed in richest green—
   The laughing stream—the willows bending o'er.
With tear dimmed eyes she views each sylvan scene,
   And thinks earth never was so fair before.

We do not sigh for Heaven, till we have known,
   Something of sorrow, something of grief and woe,
And as a summer day her life has flown.
   Then, can we wonder she is loth to go ?

She has no friends in Heaven : all are here.
   No lost one waits her in that unknown land,
And life grows doubly, trebly sweet and dear,
   As day by day she nears the mystic strand.

We love her and we grieve to see her go.
   But it is Christ who calls her to His breast,
And He shall greet her, and she soon shall know
   The joys of souls that dwell among the blest.

1869.

HAUNTED.

"We walk upon the sea-shore, you and I,
   Just two alone," you say.   But there are three ;
A tall and manly form is walking nigh,
   And as I move, he moves along with me.

Your shadow ?   No, for shadows do not speak,
   And he is speaking, tenderly and low,
Words that bring crimson blushes to my cheek,
   You cannot hear, the sea is sounding so.

But it is strange you cannot see him there,
  My darling with the broad and snowy brow.
You never saw a face so grandly fair.
  I'll stand aside—there, do you see him now ?

No ! well you jest, or else you're growing blind ;
  Blue eyes are never very strong, you know ;
This summer sun and wind are bad combined,
  You should not walk here where the sea gales blow.

Ah, he who walks here at my side has eyes
  That sun, nor wind can dim their eagle sight,
You've seen the thunder cloud in stormy skies—
  Well, so his eyes are, full of purple light.

Dead ! what a foolish thing for you to say,
  When I can see him walking at my side ;
Just as we walked a year ago to-day,
  When first I promised him to be his bride.

Go, leave us.   We had rather be alone.
  Your words are wild to-day.   Go, let me be
With him a while.   And when an hour has flown
  I'll follow you.   But now he waits for me.

GHOSTS.

There are ghosts in the room,
As I sit here alone, from the dark corners there
They come out of the gloom
And they stand at my side, and they lean on my chair.

There's the ghost of a hope
That lighted my days with a fanciful glow.
In her hand is the rope
That strangled her life out.   Hope was slain long ago.

But her ghost comes to-night,
With its skeleton face, and expressionless eyes,
And it stands in the light,
And mocks me, and jeers me with sobs and with sighs.

There's the ghost of a Joy,
A frail, fragile thing, and I prized it too much,
And the hands that destroy
Clasped it close, and it died at the withering touch.

There's the ghost of a love,
Born with joy, reared with Hope, died in pain and unrest,

But he towers above
All the others—this ghost : yet a ghost at the best.

I am weary, and fain
Would forget all these dead : but the gibbering host
Make the struggle in vain,
In each shadowy corner, there lurketh a ghost.

1869.

———

TIM'S STORY.

I was out promenading one fine summer day,
When I chanced upon three bosom cronies to stray,
And a beer shop we happened to pass on our way.

" Now boys," said I, stopping them all with a wink,
"If you'll step round the corner, I'll treat to a drink ;
How is it, my hearties ? now, what do you think ?"

So into the bar-room we dropped in a flash,
And up to the keeper I went with a dash :
" Four glasses of lager, and none of your trash,

But the best and the foamiest money can bring,"
Was the order I gave, with the air of a king ;
And mine host fluttered off, like a bird on the wing.

Just then an old toper dropped in from the street,
A jolly old soak, with a nose like a beet,
And he said, " Now, my rummys, I'll share in that treat."

But I said to my cronies, "Say boys, look ye there !
Do you 'spose such a nosey will fall to our share ?"
Quoth the toper, " Keep drinking, my lads, and you'll
    wear

A nose like my own, or I miss in my guess."
" Why," said Ned, "it resembles the light of distress."
Said Tom, " It's the color of Sally Ann's dress."

Said Billy, " It looks like the sun's ruddy bed,
And shines like the top of my grandfather's head."
Said I, "It is ready, I think, to be bled."

" Now thank ye, my lads," said old soak with a bow,
" But gulp down your lager, 'twill soon show ye how
Red noses are painted and polished, I vow."

I turned to my cronies :   "Now, boys, look ye here !
I would'nt, I say, for ten thousand a year,
Have my nose grow to look like the one beaming near !"

" Nor I, sir !" " Nor I, sir !" "Nor I !" cried each chum;
Then, said I, "A good-bye to all beer, ale, and rum,
And hurrah for cold water ! my boys, will ye come ?"

" We are ready and willing," said Tom, Bill and Ned.
" Lets get us a pledge, boys, aud sign it," I said—
And so at next meeting, four names were read

In the Temperance column.   And now should you be
In these parts, and a fine looking fellow should see,
You may know it is one of my cronies, or me.

By lectures, and preaching, some fellows are won,
But you see it is different with us : it was done
By the jolly old soak, with a nose like the sun !

1870.

MEMORY'S GARDEN.

Back on its golden hinges
  The gate of Memory swings,
And my heart goes into the garden
  And walks with the olden things.
The old-time, joys and pleasures,
  The loves that it used to know,
It meets there in the garden,
  And they wander to and fro.

It heareth a peal of laughter,
  It seeth a face most fair,
It thrills with a wild, strange rapture

At the glance of a dark eye there ;
It strayeth under the sunset
   In the midst of a merry throng,
And beats in a tuneful measure,
   To the snatch of a floating song.

It heareth a strain of music
   Swell on the dreamy air,
A strain that is never sounded,
   Save in the garden there.
It wanders among the roses,
   And thrills at a long-lost kiss,
And glows at the touch of fingers,
   In a tremor of foolish bliss.

But all is not fair in the garden,—
   There's a sorrowing sob of pain ;
There are tear-drops, bitter, scalding,
   And the roses are tempest-slain.
And I shut the gate of the garden,
   And walk in the Present's ways,
For its quiet paths are better
   Than the pain of those vanished days !

MYSTERIES.

In God's vast wisdom, infinite and grand—
Too vast, too infinite, for mortal mind—

There are some things I cannot understand.
　In all His paths, in all His ways, I find
Some subtle mysteries of life and death—
　　Some marvels that I cannot comprehend,
　　Nor can I hope to know them till the end,
When all shall be made plain, above—beneath.

There are so many of His righteous deeds—
　There is so much that unto me is plain,
I have no time to wonder—have no needs
　To question why, and wherefore.　In the main
My *mortal* eyes see that His works are good.
　　Whatever else seems strange, and dark, and dim,
　　I am content to leave in faith with Him,
And in His time it will be understood.

These labyrinths wherein many souls are lost—
　These waters, whereon some barks lose the shore,
But draw me nearer to the Heavenly Host,
　But make me love and worship God the more.
There is enough that I do see and know—
　　There is enough that I can understand,
　　And sometime Christ shall take me by the hand,
Explaining all that seems so strange below.

1870.

WHAT THE WINDS TOLD ME.

The winds come from the West,
  Come softly, mildly,
"What tidings do you bring?"
  I questioned wildly.
They sang a tender tune,
  And answered lightly—
"Your darling's path is fair!
  The sun shines brightly."

The winds came from the West,
  Came shrieking, greaning.
"What tidings now, oh wind?"
  My heart cried moaning.
They answered loud, and wild,
  "When danger stalketh—
And death is waiting, near,
  Your darling walketh."

The winds came from the West,
  Came weeping, wailing.
"Oh tell me, tell me, winds!"
  My heart cried, failing.
"Where none are near to soothe,"
  They answered sighing,
"In loneliness and pain,
  Your love is dying!"

The winds came from the West!
　Came sadly sobbing.
And with an awful fear,
　My heart was throbbing.
I wildly questioned them
　Amidst my weeping,
" All still, and white," they said,
　" Your love is sleeping."

　　　　　　　　　　1870.

———

SOMETIMES.

Sometimes when I am all alone,
　Away from noise and strife,
The many faults and weaknesses,
　That rule my daily life
Seem to die out.　And as I sit
　From worldliness apart,
All that is good and pure obtains
　The mastery of my heart.

And then my soul turns heavenward,
　And I commune with God.
I long to tread the narrow path
　That Christ before me trod.
I long to see his precious face—
　To go where angels go,

To leave the fleeting, fading things
   That make up life below.

My soul expands with ecstacy,
   My heart grows brave, and strong,
To meet whatever lies ahead—
   To battle down the wrong.
No sorrow can affright my soul,
   No earthly ill, I fear,
While in that blessed trance I sit
   And feel that God is near.

And then I mingle with the world,
   And falter day by day.
Until at last I walk within
   The olden, sinful way.
O, shall I even grow in grace,
   O shall I ever be,
Ready to meet the judgment day—
   Fit for eternity?

1869.

BLIND SORROW.

One bitter time of mourning, I remember,
   When day, and night, my sad heart did complain,
My life, I said, was one cold, bleak December,
   And all its pleasures, were but whited pain.

Nothing could rouse me from my sullen sorrow,
 Because you were not near, I would not smile.
And from a score of joys refused to borrow
 One ray of light, to gild the weary while.

But all the blessing God has given, scorning,
 I wept because we were so far apart,
And spent my time in idle, aimless mourning,
 That only kept the grief fresh in my heart.

God pity me ! I know now we were nearer,
 With all these intervening miles of space—
That life was sweeter, and the future dearer,
 Than when to-day I met you, face to face !

God meant to break it gently—ease my anguish,
 But I rebelled, and caviled at His will.
Now, seeing His great wisdom, though I languish,
 In bitter pain, I trust His mercy still.

———

"BE NOT WEARY."

Sometimes, when I am toil-worn and aweary,
 All tired out, with working long, and well,
And earth is dark, and skies above are dreary,
 And heart and soul are all too sick to tell,

These words have come to me, like angel fingers,
　Pressing the spirit eyelids down in sleep.
"Oh let us not be weary in well doing,
　For in due season we shall surely reap."

Oh blessed promise ! when I seem to hear it,
　Whispered by angel voices on the air,
It breathes new life, and courage to my spirit,
　And gives me strength to suffer and forbear.
And I can wait most patiently for harvest,
　And cast my seeds, nor ever faint, nor weep,
If I know surely, that my work availeth,
　And in God's season, I at last shall reap.

When mind and body were borne down completely
　And I have thought my efforts were all vain,
These words have come to me, so softly, sweetly,
　And whispered hope, and urged me on again.
And though my labor seems all unavailing,
　And all my strivings fruitless, yet the Lord
Doth treasure up each little seed I scatter,
　And sometime, *sometime*, I shall reap reward.

　　　　　　　　　　　　1870.

————

TO THOSE WHO NEVER PRAY.

　O ! you who never bend the knee,
　　And never lift the heart,

How do you live from year to year,
   And living, act your part.

How do you rise up in the morn,
   And pass the whole day through,
Without the Saviour at your side
   To guide and strengthen you.

How do you meet the daily ills
   That try the temper so !
That fret the heart and wear the soul
   More than some master woe.

How do you close your eyes and sleep,
   And how your crosses bear ;
(Each has a cross, or small, or large)
   Without the aid of prayer ?

How do you meet the mighty griefs,
   That rush upon the soul,
Engulfing it in bitterness,
   As angry waters roll ?

How do you live *at all*, is one
   Deep mystery to me,
Oh you who never lift the heart
   And never bend the knee.

                       1870.

HUNG.

Nine o'clock, and the sun shines as yellow and warm,
As though 'twere a fete day.   I wish it would storm :
      Wish the thunder would crash,
      And the red lightning flash,
And lap the black clouds, with its serpentine tongue—
The day is *too* calm, for a man to be hung.
      Hung ! ugh, what a word !
The most heartless, and horrible, ear ever heard.

He has murdered, and plundered, and robbed, so " they
    say,"
Been the scourge of the country, for many a day.
      He was lawless and wild ;
      Man, woman, or child
Met no mercy, no pity, if found in his path.
He was worse than a beast of the woods, in his wrath.
      And yet—to be *hung*,
      Oh my God ! to be swung
By the neck to, and fro, for the rabble to see—
      The thought sickens me.

.

Thirty minutes past nine.   How the time hurries by,
But a half hour remains, at ten he will die.
      Die ? No ! he'll be *killed !*
      For God never willed

Men should die in this way.
"Vengeance is mine," He saith, "I will repay."
        Yet what could be done,
        With this wild, lawless one !
No prison could hold him, and so—he must swing,
        It's a horrible thing.

Outcast, Desperado, Fiend, Knave ; all of these
And more.   But call him whatever you please
        I cannot forget,
        He's a mortal man yet :
That he once was a babe, and was hushed into rest,
And fondled, and pressed, to a woman's warm breast.
        Was sung to; and rocked,
        And when he first walked
With his weak little feet, he was petted, and told
He was "mamma's own pet, worth his whole weight in
        gold."
        And this is the end
Of a God-given life.   Just think of it, friend !

Hark ! hear you that chime ? 'tis the clock striking ten.
The dread weight falls down, with a sound like "amen."
Does murder pay murder ? do two wrongs make a right?
        Oh that horrible sight !
I am shut in my room, and have covered my face ;
But the dread scene has followed me into this place.
        I see that strange thing,
        Like a clock pendulum swing

To and fro, in the air, back and forth, to and fro.
        One moment ago
'Twas a man, in God's image ! now hide it, kind grave !
What a terrible end, to the life that God gave.

                    1871.

COMPASSION.

There is a picture, that I sometimes see,
  Of Jesus, with a child upon his breast.
And other children clustered at his knee—
  The little lambs of God, that he had blest.
And this one—lying on the Saviour's arm
  Looks up and smiles, in that most sainted face,
And knowing he is well secured from harm
  He falls asleep in that safe resting place.

To-night I am so weary, heart, and soul.
  So worn out, with a thousand nameless ills.
My spirit longs intensely for its goal
  And every fibre of my being thrills
With mighty yearning. "Oh to be that child—
  To lie upon my Saviour's breast." I weep,
" And looking on that face so meekly mild,
  Forget my tears, and sweetly fall asleep."

It is not always so : sometimes the earth
  And earthly friends, can satisfy my heart.

But now—to-night—I feel their shallow worth,
  And feel, oh Christ my Saviour, that Thou art
And Thou alone, the only faithful friend
  Who knowing all my sins, and seeing me
Just as I am, will pity to the end
  And in compassion, judge me tenderly.

I am so weak, and sinful—every day
  The sins and failings that I most condemn,
And most abhor in others—I straitway
  Go forth, and wickedly walk into them.
But Christ who was in mortal form one time
  And dwelt upon the earth, will understand.
And through a love and pity most sublime,
  Will write me out a pardon with His hand.

                        1869.

———

FAME.

If I should die, to-day,
 To-morrow, maybe, the world would see—
Would waken from sleep, and say,
" Why here was talent ! why here was worth !
Why here was a luminous light o' the earth.
        A soul as free
        As the winds of the sea:
        To whom was given

A dower of heaven.
And fame, and name, and glory belongs
To this dead singer of living songs.
Bring hither a wreath, for the bride of death !"
And so they would praise me, and so they would raise me
  Mayhap, a column, high over the bed
  Where I should be lying, all cold and dead.

  But I am a *living* poet !
  Walking abroad in the sunlight of God,
   Not lying asleep, where the clay worms creep,
    And the cold world will not show it,
E'en when it sees that my song should please ;
But sneering says: " Avaunt, with thy lays !
Do not sing them, and do not bring them
   Into this rustling, bustling life.
We have no time, for a jingling rhyme,
In this scene of hurrying, worrying strife."
   And so I say, there is but one way
To win me a name, and bring me fame.
And that is, to die, and be buried low,
When the world would praise me, an hour or so.

1870.

HER MOTHER'S BEAUTIFUL EYES.

I met a young girl on the street ;
  I was a stranger to her, no more.

But the glance of her brown eyes, shy and sweet,
   Set me to dreaming of days of yore.
      Ah ! *she* does not know, but long ago
When life was as cloudless as June's blue skies,
Her *mother* was all the world to me ;
      And she
Has her mother's beautiful eyes.

She lifted her lashes, and let them fall ;
   Raised them and dropped them as I past by.
A grizzled old stranger, that was all
   She saw, for she could not know that I
      In the dear, dear past
      Too sweet to last
Had found my Eden, my paradise,
In her mother's beautiful eyes.

I loved, and was loved.   But a word was said
   In thoughtless jest, and the work was done.
The hopes I had cherished, lay blasted, dead—
   My rival pleaded his suit, and won.
And their child—ah me ! is fair to see ;
I wonder if she's as good and wise,
As sweet and kind, and pure of mind
As the one who bequeathed her those beautiful eyes.

She has her father's step, and air.
   Her father's brow, and his pale, dark cheek,
And her father's tawny, curling hair,

And her father's mouth, half sweet, half weak.
    All very true.
And "she's like her father through and through,"
    I said when we met on the street that day,
    "And not like her mother in any way."
    Then I caught my breath with a start of surprise,
       (That she did not see)
For the child of my rival glanced up at me
    With her mother's beautiful eyes.

                  1871.

OLD TIMES.

Friend of my youth, let us talk of old times ;
    Of the long lost golden hours.
When "Winter" meant only Christmas chimes,
    And "Summer" wreaths of flowers.
Life has grown old, and cold, my friend,
    And the winter now, means death.
And summer blossoms speak all too plain
    Of the dear, dead forms beneath.

But let us talk of the past to-night ;
    And live it over again,
We will put the long years out of sight,
    And dream we are young as then.
But you must not look at me, my friend,
    And I must not look at you,

Or the furrowed brows, and silvered locks,
　　Will prove our dream untrue.

Let us sing of the summer, too sweet to last,
　　And yet too sweet to die.
Let us read tales, from the book of the past,
　　And talk of the days gone by.
We will turn our backs to the West, my friend,
　　And forget we are growing old.
The skies of the Present are dull, and gray,
　　But the Past's are blue, and gold.

The sun has passed over the noontide line
　　And is sinking down the West.
And of friends we knew in days Lang Syne,
　　Full half have gone to rest.
And the few that are left on earth, my friend,
　　Are scattered far, and wide.
But you and I will talk of the days
　　Ere any roamed, or died.

Auburn ringlets, and hazel eyes—
　　Blue eyes and tresses of gold.
Winds joy laden, and azure skies,
　　Belong to those days of old.
We will leave the Present's shores awhile
　　And float on the Past's smooth sea.

(But I must not look at you, my friend,
  And you must not look at me. /

THIS WORLD.

This world is a sad, sad place I know ;
  And what soul living can doubt it.
But it will not lessen the want and woe,
  To be always singing about it.
Then away with the songs that are full of tears,
  Away with dirges that sadden.
Let us make the most of our fleeting years,
  By singing the lays that gladden.

The world at its saddest is not all sad—
  There are days of sunny weather.
And the people within it are not all bad,
  But saints and sinners together.
I think those wonderful hours in June,
  Are better by far, to remember,
Than those when the world gets out of tune
  In the cold, bleak winds of November.
Because we meet in the walks of life
  Many a selfish creature,
It does not prove that this world of strife
  Has no redeeming feature.

There is bloom, and beauty upon the earth,
   There are buds and blossoming flowers,
There are souls of truth, and hearts of worth—
   There are glowing, golden hours.

In thinking over a joy we've known,
   We easily make it double.
Which is better by far, than to mope and moan,
   Over sorrow and grief and trouble.
For though this world is sad, we know,
   (And who that is living can doubt it,)
It will not lessen the want, or woe,
   To be always singing about it.

                    1872.

GOING AWAY.

Walking to-day on the Common,
   I heard a stranger say
To a friend who was standing near him,
   "Do you know I am going away?"
I had never seen their faces :
   May never see them again,
But the words the stranger uttered,
   Stirred me with nameless pain.

For I knew some heart would miss him,
   Would ache at his "going away,"

And the earth would seem all cheerless,
  For many and many a day.
No matter how glad my spirit,
  No matter how light my heart.
If I hear these two words uttered,
  The tear drops always start.

They are so sad and solemn,
  So full of a lonely sound :
Like dead leaves rustling downward,
  And dropping upon the ground.
Oh I pity the naked branches,
  When the skies are dull and gray,
And the last leaf whispers softly,
  " Good bye, I am going away."

In the dreary, dripping Autumn,
  The wings of the flying birds
As they soar away to the southland,
  Seem always to say these words.
Where ever they may be uttered,
  They fall with a sob, and sigh ;
And heart-aches follow the sentence,
  " I am going away—Good bye."

Oh God, in Thy blessed kingdom
  No lips shall ever say,
No ears shall ever hearken,
  To the words " I am going away."

For no soul ever wearies
    Of the dear, bright, angel band,
And no saint ever wanders,
    From the sunny, golden land.

1872.

GOOD BYE.

He rose, and passing, paused by her.
    They stood a moment in the door.
His dark eyes made her pulses stir
    As they had never stirred before;
How soft the night bird sang above
The dull brown heath.   Oh Life, oh Love !

He took her hand, and said " Good bye."
    Then, singing blithely, went across
The sodden fields : nor heard the cry
    Her heart sent up, nor knew her loss.
How bleak, and wild, and desolate,
The wind blew down.   Oh Love, oh Fate !

The west turned suddenly aflame ;
    Striped here and there with blue and gold.
She shook with chills she could not name.
    The air seemed strangely harsh, and cold.

How keen the winds were, and how rife
With wintry sounds.   Oh Love, oh Life !

She waited till she saw him pass
    Across the meadow, out of sight.
His shadow fell upon the grass;
    The winds were talking of the night.
How high they whirled the withered leaf ;
How swift it flew.   Oh Love, oh Grief.

She shut the door, and turned away.
    Some task was waiting for her hand.
She shut another door, where lay,
    Her sweet dead hope.   You understand.
" And they shall weep no more," God saith,
" Nor taste of pain."   Oh Life, oh Death.

JAMIE.

In through the kitchen, the boys came trooping :
    Will, and Sammy, and Bob and Fred,
And Johnny and Jamie, the twins, came after,
Setting the rafters, a-ring with laughter.
    Woe for the words I said !
I looked at the floor I had swept and dusted,
    And saw the litter the twelve feet brought ;
And I sighed, and frowned, on the six bright blossoms,
    And frowning, spoke my thought.

"Oh, was there ever so weary a woman!
   I have been only twelve years wed.
But I've never a moment of peace or quiet.
Six rough boys, with their noise and riot,
   Are wearing me out," I said.
"Six rough boys to mend and work for,
   To clothe and feed—it is hard at best;
There's never an end to my weary labors,
   There is no time for rest."

Dark fell the shadows around my little cottage,
   Weeping I leaned over one little bed,
Vain were the tears on the tiny face falling;
In the dim distance I heard a voice calling—
   "Come unto me," it said.
And down through the starlight an angel descended,
   And stood by my Jamie's low bedside.
"Come! there is room with the angels," she whispered,
   "Heaven is fair and wide."

"Fair are its meadows, and wide are its mansions,
   And thousands of children are gathered there."
Vain were the prayers that I prayed, leaning o'er him,
Up to the mansions of heaven she bore him.
   Woe for my heart's despair!
Oh, to recall the harsh words that I uttered!
   Oh, for his litter and noise to-day!
Oh, for the labor his hands would make me!
   Hands that are turned to clay.

Five sturdy boys troop into my cottage,
  John, Will, Sammy, and Bob and Fred—
Five brave boys as e'er blessed a mother.
But always and ever I miss the other,
  The dear, dear boy that is dead.
I miss the ring of his childish laughter,
  Miss him and mourn for him night and day,
But wide are the mansions, and fair are the meadows
  Where the feet of my Jamie stray.

1872.

A MOTHER'S REVERIE.

The shadows drop down o'er the fields tinged with brown,
  Where the snow-drifts were gleaming of late,
And the day shuts her eyes, while th' red western skies
  Make ready the chambers of state.
How still the house seems ! while round about gleams
  Th' last mellow rays of th' sun.
There's no step on the stair—no voice anywhere,
  Crying, "Mother, the last task is done !"

Can it be I'm alone? can it be there are none
  Left of eight, who have called me that name ?
Four boys and four girls, with their tresses and curls,
  Four brave boys, four fair girls, that came
To my home one by one, like lost rays from the sun,

4

And where are they all now? I pray;
Like birds from the nest, the babes on my breast
  Took wing, and have fluttered away.

There was John, my first child; as gentle and mild
  As the maiden that grew at his side,—
First to come, last to stay; but death called him away,—
  It is two years, to-day since he died.
Hope, Mary, and Joe are all married, and so
  Have gone into homes of their own;
Mark is over the sea, and Flora—hush! we
  Never speak of the one who has flown.

My Will, bonny Will, fell at Champion Hill—
  My dark-eyed, my raven-tressed son;
There was one at his side fell too; and Kate died
  Of grieving for Will—and that one!
Yet bravely we try, my life-mate and I,
  To be happy and cheerful alway.
God knows best what to do; yet I think if we knew
  She were dead, 'twould seem better to-day.

                                    1871.

THE TWO GLASSES.

There sat two glasses, filled to the brim,
On a rich man's table, rim to rim.

One was ruddy, and red as blood,
And one was as clear as the crystal flood.

Said the glass of wine to his paler brother,
" Let us tell tales of the past to each other ;
I can tell of banquet, and revel, and mirth,
Where I was king, for I ruled in might.
And the proudest and grandest souls on earth
Fell under my touch, as though struck with blight.
From the heads of kings I have torn the crown,
From the heights of fame I have hurled men down ;
I have blasted many an honored name,
I have taken virtue, and given shame ;
I have tempted the youth, with a sip, a taste,
That has made his future a barren waste.
Far greater than any king am I,
Or than any army beneath the sky.
I have made the arm of the driver fail,
And sent the train from its iron rail.
I have made good ships go down at sea,
And the shrieks of the lost were sweet to me ;
For they said, "Behold, how great you be !
Fame, strength, wealth, genius, before you fall,
And your might and power are over all."
"Ho ! ho ! pale brother," laughed the wine,
"Can you boast of deeds as great as mine ?"

Said the water glass, " I cannot boast
Of a king dethroned or a murdered host ;

But I can tell of hearts that were sad,
By my crystal drops made light and glad.
Of thirsts I have quenched, and brows I've laved ;
Of hands I have cooled, and souls I've saved.
I have leaped through the valley, dashed down the moun-
tain ;
Slept in the sunshine, and dripped from the fountain.
I have burst my cloud fetters, and dropped from the sky,
And everywhere gladdened the landscape and eye.
I have eased the hot forehead of fever and pain,
I have made the parched meadows grow fertile with
grain ;
I can tell of the powerful wheel o' the mill,
That ground out the flour, and turned at my will ;
I can tell of manhood, debased by you,
That I have uplifted, and crowned anew.
I cheer, I help, I strengthen and aid,
I gladden the heart of man and maid ;
I set the chained wine-captive free,
And all are better for knowing me."

These are the tales they told each other,
The glass of wine, and its paler brother,
As they sat together, filled to the brim,
On the rich man's table, rim to rim.

1872.

TWILIGHT THOUGHTS.

The God of the day has vanished
　The light from the hills has fled,
And the hand of an unseen artist,
　Is painting the West all red.
All threaded with gold and crimson,
　And burnished with amber dye,
And tipped with purple shadows,
　The glory flameth high.

Fair, beautiful world of ours !
　Fair, beautiful world, but oh,
How darkened by pain and sorrow,
　How blackened by sin and woe.
The splendor pales in the heavens
　And dies in a golden gleam,
And alone in the hush of twilight,
　I sit, in a checkered dream.

I think of the souls that are straying,
　In shadows as black as night,
Of hands that are groping blindly
　In search of the shining light ;
Of hearts that are mutely crying,
　And praying for just one ray,
To lead them out of the shadows,
　Into the better way.

I think of the Father's children
   Who are trying to walk alone,
Who have dropped the hand of the Parent,
   And wander in ways unknown.
Oh, the paths are rough and thorny,
   And I know they cannot stand.
They will faint and fall by the wayside,
   Unguided by God's right hand.

And I think of the souls that are yearning
   To follow the good and true ;
That are striving to live unsullied,
   Yet know not what to do.
And I wonder when God, the Master,
   Shall end this weary strife,
And lead us out of the shadows
   Into the deathless life.

                        1869.

ONLY A KISS.

Once, when the summer lay on the hilltops,
   And the sunshine fell like a golden flame,
Out from the city's dust and turmoil
   A gallant, fair-faced stranger came—
Came to rest in our humble cottage
   Till the winds of autumn should blow again,

To walk in the meadow and lie by the brooklet,
  And woo back the strength, that the town had slain.

I was young, with the foolish heart of a maiden
  That had never been wooed, and the stranger bland
Awoke that heart from its idle dreaming,
  And swept the strings with a master-hand.
I remember the thrill, and the first wild tremor,
  That stirred its depths with a sweet surprise,
When I glanced one day at the handsome stranger,
  And caught the gaze of his deep, dark eyes.

My cheek grew red with its tell-tale blushes,
  And the knitting dropped from my nerveless grasp ;
He stooped, and then, as he gracefully gave it,
  He held my hand in a loving clasp ;
We said no word, but he knew my secret,
  He read what lay in my maiden heart,
No vain concealing was needed longer
  To hide the tremor his voice would start.

We walked in the meadow and by the brooklet,
  My sun-browned hand in his snowy palm ;
He said my blushes would shame the roses,
  And my heart stood still in a blissful calm.
He stroked my tresses, my raven ringlets,
  And twined them over his finger fair ;
My eyes' dark splendor was full of danger,
  He said, for Cupid was lurking there.

And once he held me close to his bosom,
   And pressed on my lips a loving kiss ;
Oh ! how I tremble with shame and anger,
   Even now, as I think of this—
But in that moment I thought that heaven
   Had suddenly opened and drawn me in,
And kissed with passion the lips, so near me,
   Nor dreamed I was staining my soul with sin.

But there came a letter one quiet evening
   To the man who was dearer to me than life—
" A picture," he said, as he tore it open,
   " Look, sweet friend, at my fair young wife."
A terrible anguish, a seething anger,
   Heaved my bosom and blanched my cheek,
And he who stood there holding the letter,
   He watched me smiling, but did not speak.

I took the picture and gazed upon it—
   A sweet young creature with sunny hair
And eyes of blue. "May the good Lord keep you,"
   I said aloud, "in his tender care—
You who are wedded and bound forever
Unto this man," and I met his eyes—
" This soulless villain, this shameless coward,
   Whose heart is blackened with acted lies."

My heart swelled full of a terrible hatred,
   And something of murder was burning there,

But a better feeling stole in behind it
  As I looked on the picture sweet and fair ;
I turned and left him, and never saw him—
  Never looked on his face again,
And time has tempered my shame and sorrow,
  And soothed and quieted down my pain.

But I always tremble, in awful anger,
  That wears and worries my waning life,
When I think how he clasped me close to his bosom,
  He—with a lawfully wedded wife.
When I think how I answered his fond caresses,
  And clung to his neck in a trance of bliss,
And the tears of a life time and all my sorrow,
  Can never remove the stain of his kiss.

                                    1869.

WHEN I AM DEAD.

When I am dead, if some chastened one,
  Seeing the "item," or hearing it said
That my play is over, and my part done,
  And I lie asleep in my narrow bed—
If I could know that some soul would say,
  Speaking aloud or silently,
"In the heat, and burden of the day,
  She gave a refreshing draught to me ;"

Or, "when I was lying nigh unto death,
　　She nursed me to life, and to strength again,
And when I labored and struggled for breath,
　　She soothed and quieted down my pain ;"
Or, "when I was groping in grief and doubt,
　　Lost, and turned from the light o' the day,
Her hand reached me and helped me out,
　　And led me up to the better way ;"

Or, "when I was hated and shunned by all,
　　Bowing under my sin and my shame,
She, once, in passing me by, let fall
　　Words of pity and hope that came
Into my heart, like a blessed calm
　　Over the waves of the stormy sea,
Words of comfort like oil and balm,
　　She spake, and the desert blossomed for me ;"

Better by far, than a marble tomb—
　　Than a monument towering over my head ;
(What shall I care, in my quiet room,
　　For head board or foot board, when I am dead)
Better than glory, or honors, or fame,
　　(Though I am striving for those to-day)
To know that some heart will cherish my name,
　　And think of me kindly, with blessings, alway.

1870.

DON'T TALK WHEN YOU'VE NOTHING TO SAY.

It is well to be free in conversing,
    It is well to be able to chat
With a friend on a subject of interest—
    With a stranger on this thing or that.
Don't aim to be cold or reticent,
    But listen to reason I pray,
And remember this wisest of mottos,
    "Don't talk when you've nothing to say."

A gay, lively friend, or companion,
    With wits that are ready and quick,
Is better by far, than a stupid,
    And unconversational stick.
Yet speech at the best is but silver,
    While silence is golden alway.
And remember at all times and places,
    Don't talk when you've nothing to say.

I like to see well informed people
    Who know *what* to say, *how* and *when*.
And a little good nonsense and jesting
    Is not out of place, now and then.
But I dread the approach of a Magpie,
    Who chatters from grave themes to gay,
Who talks from the morn to the midnight,
    And always with nothing to say.

1871.

THE FROST FAIRY.

All day the trees were moaning
    For the leaves that they had lost,
All day they creaked and trembled,
    And the naked branches tossed
And shivered in the north wind
    As he hurried up and down,
Over hill-tops bleak and cheerless,
    Over meadows bare and brown.

"Oh my green and tender leaflets.
    Oh my fair buds, lost and gone !"
So they moaned through all the daytime,
    So they groaned till night came on.
And the hoar-frost lurked and listened
    To the wailing, sad refrain,
And he whispered, "wait—be patient—
    I will cover you again ;

I will deck you in new garments—
    I will clothe you ere the light,
In a sheen of spotless glory—
    In a robe of purest white.
You shall wear the matchless mantle,
    That the good Frost Fairy weaves."
And the bare trees listened, wondered,
    And forgot their fallen leaves.

And the quaint and silent fairy,
   Backward, forward, through the gloom,
Wove the matchless, glittering mantle,
   Spun the frost-thread on her loom.
And the bare trees talked together,
   Talked in whispers soft and low,
As the good and silent fairy
   Moved her shuttle to and fro.

And lo ! when the golden glory
   Of the morning crept abroad,
All the trees were clothed in grandeur,
   All the twiglets robed, and shod
With matchless, spotless garments,
   That the sunshine decked with gems,
And the trees forgot their sorrow,
   'Neath their robes and diadems.

1871.

FLORABELLE.

Did you see Florabelle ? has she passed you this morn-
     ing ?
  A tall, slender Maiden, with hair like spun gold.
She has ? then I pray you, dear sir, heed my warning,
  It is just the old, oft rehearsed story re-told :

Florabelle is a jilt—a coquette—a deceiver.
　She angles for hearts, with soft words and sweet smiles.
Forewarned is forearmed, don't you trust or believe her,
　Be deaf to her cooing, be blind to her wiles.

She has eyes, like the heart of a blue morning glory,
　She has lips like a rose-bud just sprinkled with dew,
"Tis the old hackneyed tale, 'tis the same wretched story,
　A woman all fair, yet all false, and untrue.

With her soft silken hair, in its meshes and tangles,
　With her pink and white cheek, and her full ruby lips,
With her eyes shining clear, like the heavens bright
　　sparkles,
　She has wrecked as strong *hearts* as the ocean has
　　ships.

Those blue eyes are ever on watch for a stranger;
　She thirsts for fresh conquests, and she has marked
　　you,
I warn you, my friend, that your peace is in danger,
　Take heed, lest the day that you met her, you rue.

Don't bask in her smiles, for one moment, but leave
　　her,
　Before you're entangled, and find it too late.
Florabelle is a jilt—a coquet—a deceiver,
　I have given you warning ! now choose your own fate !
　　　　　　　　　　　　　　1871.

THE DOOMED CITY'S PRAYER.

(After the Burning of Chicago.)

I heard a low sound, like a troubled soul praying :
    And the winds of the winter night brought it to me.
Twas the doomed city's voice : "Oh, kind snow," it was
       saying,
    "Come, cover my ruins, so ghastly to see,
I am robbed of my beauty, and shorn of my glory ;
    And the strength that I boasted—where is it to-day ?
I am down in the dust ; and my pitiful story
    Make tearless eyes weep, and unpious lips pray.

               .

"I—I, who have reveled in pomp and in power,
    Am down on my knees, with my face in the dust.
But yesterday queen, with a queen's royal dower,
    To-day I am glad of a crumb or a crust.
But yesterday reigning, a grand mighty city,
    The pride of the nation, the queen of the West;
To-day I am gazed at, an object of pity,
    A charity child, asking alms, at the best.

"My strength, and my pride, and my glory departed,
    My fair features scorched by the fire fiends breath,
Is it strange that I'm soul-sick and sorrowful hearted ?
    Is it strange that my thoughts run on ruin and death ?
Oh, white, fleecy clouds that are drooping above me,
    Hark, hark to my pleadings, and answer my sighs,

And let down the beautiful snow, if you love me,
  To cover my wounds from all pitying eyes.

" I am hurled from my throne, but not hurled down for-
      ever,
  I shall rise from the dust, I shall live down my woes—
But my heart lies to-day, like a dumb, frozen river ;
  When to thaw out and flow again, God only knows.
Oh, sprites of the air!   I beseech you to weave me
  A mantle of white snow, and beautiful rime
To cover my unsightly ruins ; then leave me
  In the hands of the healer of all wounds—'Old
      Time.' "

                                    ·   November, 1871.

ONE WOMAN'S PLEA.

Now God be with the men who stand
    In Legislative halls, to-day.
Those chosen princes of our land—
    May God be with them all, I say,
And may His wisdom, guide, and shield them,
    For mighty is the trust we yield them.

Oh men ! who hold a people's fate,
    There in the hollow of your hand.
Each word you utter, soon, or late,

Shall leave its impress on our land,—
Forth from the halls of legislation,
    Shall speed its way, through all the Nation.

Then may The Source of Truth, and Light,
    Be ever o'er you, ever near.
And may He guide each word aright ;
    May no false precept, greet the ear,
No selfish love, for purse, or faction,
    Stay *Justices'* hand, or guide one action.

And may no one, among these men
    Lift to his lips, the damning glass,
Let no man say, with truth, again,
    What *has been* said, in truth, alas,
"Men drink, in halls of legislation—
    Why shouldn't we, of lower station !"

Oh men ! you see, you hear this beast,
    This fiend that pillages the earth,
Whose work is death—whose hourly feast,
    Is noble souls, and minds of worth—
You see—and if you will not chain him,
    Nor reach one hand forth, to detain him,

For God's sake, do not give him aid,
    Nor urge him onward.   Oh to me,
It seems so strange that laws are made
5

To crush all other crimes, while he
Who bears down through Hell's gaping portals
   The countless souls, of rum wrecked mortals,

Is left to wander, to, and fro,
   In perfect freedom through the land.
And those who *ought* to see, and know,
   Will lift no warning voice, or hand.
Oh men in halls of legislation,
   Rise to the combat, save the Nation !

                         January, 1871.

DECORATION POEM.

Gather them out of the valley—
   Bring them from moorland and hill,
And cast them in wreaths and in garlands,
   On the city so silent and still—
   So voiceless, so silent, and still ;
Where neighbor speaks never to neighbor,
   Where the song of the bird, and the brown bee is
      heard,
But never the harsh sounds of labor.

Bring them from woodland and meadow—
   As fresh, and as fair, as can be.
Bring them, all kinds, and all colors,

That grow upon upland and lea—
    That spring in wild grace on the lea.
And rifle the green earth's warm bosom
    Of each flower, and blow, till "God's acre" shall glow
And bloom, like a garden in blossom. ·

Bring them from vase, and from hot-house,
    And strew them with bountiful hand.
There is nothing too rare for the soldier,
    Who laid down his life for his land—
    Who laid down *all things* for his land ;
And turned to the duty before him,
    And how now can we prove, our thanks and our love
But by casting these May blossoms o'er him.

We know they will soon fade, and wither—
    We know they will soon droop, and die ;
But one time, I read, how an angel
    Came down from the mansions on high—
    In the night, from God's kingdom on high—
Came down where a poor faded flower
    Lay crushed by rude feet, in the dust of the street,
And he carried it up to God's bower ;

And laid it before the Good Master,
    Who kissed it, and passed it to Christ,
On the throne at His side ; and *He* kissed it,
    And the touch of those kisses sufficed—
    The caress of the God-head sufficed—

And it bloomed out in wonderful splendor,
　　A thing of delight, and most fair in God's sight—
'Tis a fable, I know ; but *so* tender ;

So sweet that I like to believe it—
　　And I have been thinking, to-day,
That mayhap these soldiers, now angels,
　　Will come, when these wreathes fade away—
　　When they wither, and shrivel away—
And will bear the crushed things up to heaven,
　　And God, and His Son. will kiss them, each one,
And new beauty, and bloom will be given.

And odd fancy, perhaps, yet dispute it,
　　And *prove* it untrue if you can.
There are strange, subtle ways, in God's workings
　　Now veiled from the knowledge of man,
　　Shut out from the vision of man.—
By a dark veil of deep, mortal blindness ;
　　But when God deems it right, He will give us our
　　　　sight,
And remove the thick veil, in His kindness ;

And when we have entered His kingdom,
　　And all his strange ways understand,
Who knows but these very same flowers,
　　We shall find there abloom, in His land,
　　All fresh, and all fair, in His land ;

And these soldiers, who went on before us,
 As we wander and stray, through God's gardens, shall
   say :
"These are the wreathes you cast o'er us."

Then, strew ye the best, and the brightest
 Of buds, and of blossoms full blown,
Over the graves, of the loved ones—
 Over those labelled "Unknown !"
 Oh ! the pathos of that word, "Unknown !"
Bring hither the brightest, and rarest !
 We reck not, if the clay, wore the blue garb, or gray !
We will give them the best, and the fairest.

For somebody mourned for the "missing,"
 And wept for them hot, scalding tears,
And hoped against hope, for their coming ;
 And watched, and waited, months and years,
 Such long, and such desolate years !
But the hearts are *so* patient, that love them,
 And some now watch and weep, for the soldiers who
   sleep
With the slab labeled " Unknown" above them.

Then gather from meadow, and woodland,
 From garden, and hot-house, and vase,
The brightest and choicest of blossoms,
 And scatter them here in this place ;
 This holy and hallowed place —

This city of rest, not of labor,
　　Where only the bird, and th' brown bee is heard,
And neighbor, speaks never to neighbor.

　　　Forest Hill Cemetery, May 30, 1871.

　　　———

A BABY IN THE HOUSE.

I knew that a baby was hid in that house,
　　Though I saw no cradle, and heard no cry,
But the husband went tiptoeing 'round like a mouse,
　　And the good wife was humming a soft lullaby;
And there was a look on the face of that mother
That I knew could mean only *one* thing, and no other.

"The *mother*," I said to myself; for I knew
　　That the woman before me was certainly that,
For there lay in the corner a tiny cloth shoe,
　　And I saw on a stand such a wee little hat;
And the beard of the husband said plain as could be,
"Two fat, chubby hands have been tugging at me."

And he took from his pocket a gay picture book,
　　And a dog that would bark if you pulled on a string;
And the wife laid them up with such a pleased look;
　　And I said to myself, "There is no other thing

But a babe that could bring about all this, and so
That one is in hiding here somewhere, I know."

I stayed but a moment, and saw nothing more,
   And heard not a sound, yet I knew I was right ;
What else could the shoe mean that lay on the floor—
   The book and the toy, and the faces so bright ?
And what made the husband as still as a mouse ?
I am sure, *very* sure, there's a babe in that house.

1872.

POEM.

[Read at the Reunion of the Society of the "Grand Army of the
Tennessee," at Madison, Wisconsin, July 4th, 1872.]

After the battles are over,
   And the war drums cease to beat,
And no more is heard on the hillside
   The sound of hurrying feet,
Full many a noble action,
   That was done in the days of strife,
By the soldier is half forgotten,
   In the peaceful walks of life.

Just as the tangled grasses,
   In summer's warmth and light,
Grow over the graves of the fallen

And hide them away from sight,
So many an act of valor,
  And many a deed sublime,
Fades from the mind of the soldier,
  O'ergrown by the grass of time.

Not so should they be rewarded,
  Those noble deeds of old ;
They should live forever and ever,
  When the heroes' hearts are cold.
Then rally, ye brave old comrades,
  Old veterans, re-unite !
Up root time's tangled grasses—
  Live over the march, and the fight.

Let Grant come up from the White House,
  And clasp each brother's hand,
First chieftain of the army,
  Last chieftain of the land.
Let him rest from a nation's burdens,
  And go, in thought, with his men,
Through the fire and smoke of Shiloh,
  And save the day again.

This silent hero of battles,
  Knew no such word as *defeat.*
It was left for the rebels learning,
  Along with the word retreat.
He was not given to *talking,*

But he found that guns would preach
In a way that was more convincing
　　Than fine and flowery speech.

Three cheers for the grave commander
　　Of the grand old Tennessee !
Who won the first great battle—
　　Gained the first great victory.
His motto was always "Conquer,"
　　"Success" was his countersign,
And "though it took all summer,"
　　He kept fighting upon "that line."

Let Sherman, the stern old General,
　　Respond to the reveille,
Let him march with his boys through Georgia,
　　From "Atlanta down to the sea."
Oh, that grand old tramp to Savannah !
　　Three hundred miles to the coast !
It will live in the heart of the Nation,
　　Forever its pride and boast.

As Sheridan went to the battle,
　　When a score of miles away,
*He has come to the feast and banquet,
　　By the iron horse to-day.
Its space is not much swifter
　　Than the pace of that famous steed

That bore him down to the contest
　　And saved the day by his speed.

Then go over the ground to-day, boys,
　　Tread each remembered spot.
It will be a gleesome journey,
　　On the swift-shod feet of thought;
You can fight a bloodless battle,
　　You can skirmish along the route,
But it's not worth while to forage,
　　There are rations enough without.

Don't start if you hear the cannon;
　　It is not the sound of doom,
It does not call to the contest—
　　To the battle's smoke and gloom.
"Let us have Peace," was spoken,
　　And lo! peace ruled again;
And now the nation is shouting,
　　Through the cannon's voice, "Amen."

Oh, boys, who besieged old Vicksburg,
　　Can time e'er wash away
The triumph of her surrender,
　　Nine years ago to-day?
Can you ever forget the moment,
　　When you saw that flag of white,
That told how the grim old city
　　Had fallen in her might?

Ah, 'twas a bold, brave army,
　　When the boys with a right good will,
Went gayly marching and singing
　　To the fight at Champion Hill.
They met with a warm reception,
　　But the soul of "Old John Brown"
Was abroad on that field of battle,
　　And our flag did NOT go down.

Come, heroes of Look Out Mountain,
　　Of Corinth and Donelson,
Of Kenesaw and Atlanta,
　　And tell how the day was won!
Hush! bow the head for a moment—
　　There are those who cannot come.
No bugle call can arouse them—
　　No sound of fife, or drum.

McPherson fell in the battle,
　　When its waves were surging high,
Brave Ransom sank by the wayside ;
　　'Twas a lonely death to die.
They walk God's fair, green meadows,
　　They dwell in a land of bliss,
Yet I think their spirits are with us
　　In such an hour as this.

Oh, boys who died for the country,
　　Oh, dear and sainted dead !

What can we say about you
    That has not once been said ?
Whether you fell in the contest,
    Struck down by shot and shell,
Or pined 'neath the hand of sickness,
    Or starved in the prison cell—

We know that you died for Freedom,
    To save our land from shame,
To rescue a periled Nation,
    And we give you deathless fame.
'Twas the cause of Truth and Justice
    That you fought and perished for,
And we say it, oh, so gently,
    "Our boys who died in the war."

Saviours of our Republic,
    Heroes who wore the blue,
We owe the peace that surrounds us—
    And our Nation's strength, to you.
We owe it to you that our banner,
    The fairest flag in the world
Is to-day unstained, unsullied,
    On the summer air unfurled.

We look on its stripes and spangles,
    And our hearts are filled the while
With love for the brave commanders,
    And the boys of the rank and file.

The grandest deeds of valor,
    Were never written out,
The noblest acts of virtue,
    The world knows nothing about.

And many a private soldier,
    Who walks his humble way,
With no sounding name or title,
    Unknown to the world to-day,
In the eyes of God is a hero ;
    All such he will reward,
No deed however secret,
    Is hidden from the Lord.

Brave men of a mighty army,
    We extend you friendships hand !
I speak for the "Loyal Women,"
    Those pillars of our land.
We wish you a hearty welcome,
    We are proud that you gather here
To talk of old times together
    On this brightest day in the year.

And if peace, whose snow white pinions,
    Brood over our land to-day,
Should ever again go from us,
    (God grant she may ever stay).
Should our Nation call in her peril
    For "Six hundred thousand more,"

The loyal women would hear her,
And send you out as before.

We would bring out the treasured knapsack.
We would take the sword from the wall,
And hushing our own heart's pleadings,
Hear only the country's call.
For next to our God, is our Nation :
And we cherish the honored name,
Of the bravest of all brave armies
Who fought for that Nation's fame.

* This stanza was written after arriving at the hall, and finding
Sheridan among the Generals present, which may serve as an explain-
ation for the change of *tense* in that verse. Not knowing that General
Sheridan was a member of the Society, no mention had been made of
him when the poem was written.

THE PEOPLE'S FAVORITE.

[A tribute to Ex-Governor Fairchild.]

God bless the hero of my song !
Six years the chieftain of our State !
We've held him, in our hearts, so long,
And proved him good, and true, and great.
That now, we could not let him go,
Even if he would have it so.

I hear the praises of his name
From east and west, and north and south,

His foes are silenced from sheer shame :
  His deeds have silenced Slander's mouth,
And all the little imps of spite
He's crushed beneath the heel of Right.

He dropped an arm one bloody day,
  In beating down the walls of wrong,
But no strength went with it away ;
  His other grew full thrice as strong.
Few men, with their two hands, have done
As noble deeds as he with one.

His soul speaks through his eye of blue,
  And all men know him one to trust,
Because his heart is kind and true,
  And all his actions prove him just.
I speak for thousands when I cry,
" The people's favorite for aye !"

May God be with him all his days—
  With him and all he holds most dear ;
And if my little song of praise
  Should chance to fall upon his ear,
May he accept the offering,
And know that from my heart I sing.

1872.

DREAM-TIME.

Throughout these mellow autumn days,
All sweet and dim, and soft with haze,
I argue with my unwise heart,
That fain would choose the idler's part.

My heart says, " Let us lie and dream
Under the sunshine's softened beam.
This is the dream-time of the year,
When Heaven itself seems bending near.

See how the calm still waters lie
And dream beneath the arching sky.
The sun draws on a veil of haze,
And dreams away these golden days.

Put by the pen—lay thought aside,
And cease to battle with the tide,
Let us, like Nature, rest and dream
And float with th' current of the stream."

So pleads my heart. I answer " Nay,
Work waits for you and me to-day.
Behind these autumn hours of gold,
The winter lingers, bleak and cold.

And those who dream too long or much,
Must waken, shivering, at his touch,
With naught to show for vanished hours,
But dust of dreams and withered flowers.

So now, while days are soft and warm,
We must make ready for the storm."
Thus, through the golden, hazy weather,
My heart and I converse together.

And yet, I dare not turn my eyes
To pebbly shores or tender skies,
Because I am so fain to do
E'en as my heart pleads with me to.

October, 1872.

LINES WRITTEN UPON THE DEATH OF JAMES BUELL.

Something is missing from the balmy spring.
  There is no perfume in its gentle breath ;
And there are sobs in songs the wild birds sing,
  And all the bees chant of the grave and death.
Something is missing from the earth.   One morn
  The angels called a new name on the roll ;
A spirit soldier to their ranks was borne,
  And all Christ's army welcomed the pure young soul.

6

He died.   Two little words, but only God
   Can understand the awful depths of woe
They hold for those who pass beneath the rod,
   Praying for strength, from Him who aimed the blow.
He died.   The soldier who fought long and well,
   Who walked with Death upon the battle-field,
Among the bellowing guns—the shrieking shell—
   In poison prison dens—and would not yield.

A six month three times told, he languished there,
   And yet he lived; oh, young heart, strong and brave!
Thank God, who heard the oft repeated prayer;
   Thank God, he does not fill a Southern grave;
That when he died, the loved ones gathered round,
   And eased the anguish of those last, sad hours.
That gentle hands can keep the precious mound
   All green with mosses, and abloom with flowers.

He was so young and fair ; and life was sweet.
   Christ give the mourners strength to drain the cup !
He went to make the Heavenly ranks complete,
   God sent the angel Death, to bear him up.
So young, and fair and brave ; beloved by all ;
   The lisping child—life's veteran, bent and gray—
And eyes grow dim, and bitter tear-drops fall
   Upon the mound where lies the soldier's clay.

Oh ! it is sweet to feel that God knows best,
   Who called in youth this brother, friend and son,

And sweet to lean upon the Saviour's breast,
  And looking upward, say, " Thy will be done."
But something is missing from the balmy spring ;
  There is no perfume in its gentle breath,
And there are sobs in songs the wild birds sing,
  And all the bees chant of the grave, and death.

UNDER THE WILLOW.

Under the willow, you and I
Walked in the gloaming, when love ran high ;
That wild first love, that was almost pain,
That we never on earth can know again.

The winds were soft, and the night was calm ;
You held my hand in your throbbing palm.
With the fire of passion your dark eyes glowed,
And the tide of my pulses madly flowed.

You drew me closely against your side—
You asked me softly to be your bride.
I trembled, and flushed, and could not speak,
But you knew my answer, and kissed my cheek.

" When earth has perished, and time is dead,
Our love will still live on," we said.

" It shall have a steady and quenchless ray,
Though youth and strength, and life decay."

The night-bird warbled a song just then ;
It sounded to us like a glad amen,
As we built our castles, and made our vows,
Under the willow's drooping boughs.

* * * * *

Under the willows, to and fro
We walked in the gloaming, when love ran low.
The tide had ebbed, the current dried,
And our wild, mad passion had slowly died.

I know not wherefore, but widely apart
We had steadily drifted, heart from heart.
Something invisible came between—
I know not what—it was fate, I ween.

The scales had dropped from our youthful eyes,
And we viewed each other in strange surprise ;
And she you deemed an angel before,
You found was a woman—and nothing more.

And the idol I worshiped for gold, alway,
I found was the poorest kind of clay.
And so it perished, at one cold breath,
The passion we said would live through death.

And under the willow again we strayed,
And sundered the vows that once were made.
We felt no sorrow—we knew no woe—
Since *love* had perished, 'twere better so.

We have dreamt our dream, we have reached the end.
You said so calmly, "farewell, my friend."
The night-bird uttered a wailing cry ;
It sounded to me like a last good-bye.

I am glad that we sundered our vows, that night.
My pathway is pleasant, my heart is light.
But I feel, my friend, as the days flow on,
That something of youth from my life is gone.

And never, on earth, can we know again,
That first, mad passion, so near to pain,
When under the willow, you and I
Walked in the gloaming, and love ran high.

DOUBTING.

Sometimes we mortals, writhing in bitter anguish,
   Crushed by great griefs, that seem too hard to bear,
And led to doubt God's goodness and his wisdom,
   And will not lift our burdened hearts in prayer.

I think these moments are the very darkest,
　　The blackest and the coldest that we know,
And I think God, and Christ, and all the angels,
　　Pity us most, in this phase of our woe.

I had a little child I fondly cherished ;
　　A winsome, playful, tender-hearted boy,
Strong willed, yet gentle, gay, yet mild and loving,
　　He was our household idol and our joy.
We lavished on him stores of pure affection ;
　　We gave him the best love our hearts possessed,
We dressed him in rich robes of finest texture,
　　And gazing on him, felt this earth life-blest.

We taught him all things good, and true, and noble ;
　　We told him of the dear Lord crucified ;
We planned for him a bright and happy future ;
　　We guarded him from danger—yet he died.
Not all the gold and riches we might lavish,
　　Not all our gold could save him from the tomb.
He died ! and when the sweet eyes closed forever,
　　They shut the sunshine in, and left but gloom.

To-day I saw a drunkard's child—a vagrant ;
　　Ill-clad, ill-fed, uncombed, unwashed, and wild ;
His home the street—his lessons vice and sorrow—
　　His garments rags—his youthful lips defiled
With rum, tobacco, lies and loud blaspheming ;

What can his future be, but one of crime ?
And thinking of this, and of my boy who slumbered,
   My heart felt hard, just for a little time.

It seemed so strange, that he, a homeless vagrant,
   Unloved, unloving, treading the road to sin,
That he was spared ; and mine so fondly cherished—
   Mine so beloved, whose life seemed so twined in
And round our heart strings, that when he was taken,
   It left them torn and bleeding—he should die ;
Ah me, it seemeth strange ; and yet God's wisdom
   I can not doubt, nor must I question why.

He, being all-wise, Father, King, Creator,
   It would be strange, if you, or I should know
All that He knows, or understand His wisdom,
   All things He does, or why He does them so.
Were all this plain, unto our mortal vision,
   There would be nothing new to learn above;
So, though the cross be great, and the prize hidden,
   I need not doubt His wisdom or His love.

                        1871.

AT SUNSET.

   I sit at my cottage window,
     In the light of the sun's last rays,
   And the hill-tops glow with splendor,

And the west is all ablaze.
My room is flooded with glory,
  My soul, with a wild delight,
And my heart is filled with poems,
  That I can not speak, or write.

O, darker, and deeper, and grander,
  The glory flames on high,
And I trace the walls of a city,
  In that beautiful western sky :
A city all gold and crimson—
  All purple and amber red ;
And the streets are paved with crystal.
  Where the feet of angels tread.

O, soulless pen and pencil.
  Thy efforts are weak and vain ;
The pen of the poet falters,
  And his heart is full of pain :
And the artist drops his pencil,
  And weeps in mute despair,
For he cannot paint the glory
  That lies in the sunset there.

But the city fadeth—fadeth ;
  The glory turns to grey ;
The golden lights are dying,
  And the splendor melts away.

And I know it was only the shadow
 Of the city built on high—
Only the poor, pale shadow,
 That I saw in the sunset sky.

And I long for that other city—
 The city that God hath made,
Where the glory never paleth,
 And the splendors never fade.
O, there at the feet of Jesus,
 In anthems of praise, I know
My soul shall utter the poems
 That fill it to overflow.

1869.

A TWILIGHT THOUGHT.

The sweet maid, Day, has pillowed her head
 On the breast of her dusky lover, Night;
The sun has made her a couch of red,
 And woven a cover of dim twilight;
And the lover kisses the maiden's brow,
As low on her couch she sleepeth now.

Here at my window, above the street,
 I sit, as the day lies in repose;
And I list to the ceaseless tramp of feet.

And I watch this human tide that flows,
Upward and downward, to and fro,
As the waves of an ocean, ebb and flow.

Over and over the busy town,
   Hither and thither, through all the day ;
One goes up, and another down—
   Each in his own alloted way.
Strangers and kinsmen pass and meet,
And jar, and jostle upon the street.

People that never met before—
   People that never will meet again :
A careless glance of the eye—no more,
   And both are lost in the sea of men.
Strangers, divided by *miles* in heart,
Under my window meet and part.

But whether their feet pass up, or down,
   Over the river, east or west,
Whether it's in or out of the town,
   To a haunt of sin, or a home of rest,
We are journeying to a common goal—
There is one last point for every soul.

Strangers and kinsmen, friend and foe,
   Whether their aims are great or small,
Whether their paths lie high, or low—

There is one last resting place for all.
Then upward, and downward, go surging by—
Under my window—you *all* must die.

1870.

————

TRUE WARRIORS.

Not always those who walk on steadily,
   In the straight path, where martyr's feet have trod,
Whose raiments seem of spotless purity,
   Not always are they most beloved of God.
Although he sees, and knows their righteousness,
   And from his throne, with loving eyes, looks down,
And hovers near, to comfort and to bless,
   And holds for each fair brow a starry crown—

Yet there are those, who sometimes wander out
   Into forbidden paths of sin, and grief,
Who sometimes hover on the brink of doubt,
   Crying, " Oh God, help thou mine unbelief !"
Whose lives are one long battle with their sins,
   Who long for righteousness, yet cling to earth ;
And he who battles thus, and battling wins,
   God holds, and prizes, as of truer worth.

For greater is he, fighting this good fight,
   Falling repeatedly, and prone to wrong,

Than he who walketh calmly in the light,
  And never falls, because he is so strong.
Who never sins, because sin tempts him not.
  To him who fights temptation one by one,
How sweet God's words when the last fight is fought,
  " Beloved servant, well, and nobly done."

1870.

ONE OF THESE.

Some have robes, of silk and velvet,
  Cast like manna, down ;
Others toil through wind and weather,
  For a homespun gown.
Some are born to ride in coaches,
  Sitting at their ease ;
Others plod foot-sore and weary.
  (I am one of these.)

Some have sounding name and title,
  Here upon the earth ;
Others dwell apart from glory—
  No one knows their worth.
Some have wealth, and fame, and beauty,
  All the things that please ;
Some are poor, and plain and lonely.
  (I am one of these.)

Some complain, in midst of pleasures,
  Of a hard, sad lot,
Doubting God, denying heaven,
  Loving, trusting not.
Others, hedged about with sorrows,
  Do, on bended knees,
Praise and bless the Lord forever.
  (I am one of these.)

A FANCY.

Drop down the crimson curtains,
  And shut out the dazzling snow,
The cold white mantle that covers
  The hills, where the grasses should grow ;
And stir up the fire till it burneth,
  With a heat like the midsummer sun.
And hang up the cage by the window,
  And bring in the plants, one by one,

Till they perfume the air with a fragrance
  As rare as the summer can bring.
And call to the bird, till he trilleth
  The sweetest of notes he can sing.
And let me lie here, while you fan me,
  Till the lazy air stirs, like a breeze,

That comes o'er the hills in the summer,
   And rustles the tops of the trees.

Then sing me a song of the summer,
   A song full of warmth and sunlight,
And I will forget that the winter
   Stalks over the earth in his might.
I will dream that I lie in the clover,
   And your voice is the voice of the breeze,
And the bird in the cage is the robin,
   That sends down his song from the trees.

1871.

———

TIRED.

My heart and soul are all to tired to tell ;
   So weary, Lord,
Of this long, ceaseless work of doing well,
   Without reward.

Oh, I have been thy servant now for years,
   Nor made complaint,
Though my life cup has been abrim with tears,
   But now I faint.

And I have worked for thee, with all my strength,
   In pain and woe.

My Master, canst thou chide me, if at length
    I ask to go?

Oh, if the soul is purified by fire,
    Then I am blest.
The laborer is worthy of his hire—
    Lord, give me rest.

I know that I have sinned in many ways—
    A sinner made.
But I have *tried* to serve thee all my days—
    I'm not afraid.

I know full well my record is not clear,
    Nor white as snow ;
But better meet it than to linger here.
    Lord, let me go.

NEVER.

I said, last winter, " When the grasses grow,
  And there are flowers abloom in every place,
And soft south winds have melted all the snow,
  Then I shall meet my darling face to face ;
And I shall clasp, and hold her hand in mine,
And I shall see her blue eyes glow and shine.

And now the grass is green on moor and lea ;
   The snow has vanished, and the spring is here,
The robins shout from every forest tree,
   The meadow larks are singing loud and clear,
And there are flowers abloom in every place—
And yet I do not see my darling's face.

All soft and mild, the gentle south wind blew,
   The snow clouds vanished, and the sunshine fell
Upon the meadow, and the daisies grew,
   And violets and pansies graced the dell.
The bees are busy, while they softly hum,
   And yet—and yet—my darling does not come.

Alas ! for never will she come again,
   She sleepeth, sleepeth, still and silent now ;
Her couch is hollowed from the grassy plain,
   And daisies bloom and blow above her brow ;
And I can never hold her hand in mine,
And I can never see her blue eyes shine.

1869.

TRUE LOVE.

I think true love is something like a tree ;
   The oak, that lifts its branches to the sky.

The woodman's axe may strike it fatally,
  Or it may fall, when mighty winds sweep by.
And where it grew, the flowers may bloom instead,
And all may seem as though the tree were dead.

But underneath the grass, and flowers, there lies,
  Hid from the gaping world, a tiny root,
A little living germ, that never dies ;
  And ever and anon its branches shoot
Up through the earth, and mock, and strive to be
The mighty forest king— the parent tree.

So love may wither, at the hand of Fate,
  Or fall beneath the killing winds that blow ;
And other loves may spring up, soon or late,
  And flowers of forgetfulness may grow,
Over the spot where love once grew instead,
And we may think the old-time passion dead.

And still the little germ lies in the heart,
  So closely hidden that it is not known ;
And ever and anon its branches start—
  Vain mimics of the passion that has flown.
Though love, once slain, can live not, as of yore,
I think its ghost will haunt us evermore.

1871.

HIS SONG.

A poet wandered the city street,
With tattered garments, and aching feet ;
Want and hunger had dimmed his eye,
And the children jeered him, as he passed by.

But one of the children sang, at play,
A song his mother had sung that day.
The poet listened, with cheeks aflame,
For the song was his own, and this was fame !

But his heart was lightened.   The song of the boy
Had thrilled the strings, with a strange, sweet joy.
" Though I may lie with the nameless dead,
The songs I have written will live," he said.

1872.

WHEN YOU GO AWAY.

When you go away, my friend,
   When we say our last good-bye,
Then the summer time will end,
   And the winter will be nigh.
Though the green grass decks the heather,
   And the birds sing all the day,

SHELLS.

There will be no summer weather,
   After you have gone away.

When I look into your eyes,
   I shall thrill with sharpest pain ;
Thinking that beneath the skies,
   I may never look again.
You will feel a moment's sorrow—
   I shall feel a lasting grief;
You forgetting on the morrow—
   I, to mourn with no relief.

When we say the last, sad words,
   And you are no longer near,
All the winds, and all the birds,
   Can not keep the summer here.
Life will lose its full completeness,
   Lose it, not for you, but me ;
All the beauty and the sweetness
   Earth can hold, I shall not see.

1870.

BLEAK WEATHER.

Dear love, where the red lillies blossomed and grew,
    The white snows are falling ;
And all through the wood, where I wandered with you,

The loud winds are calling ;
And the robin that piped to us tune upon tune,
Neath the elm—you remember,
Over tree-top and mountain has followed the June,
And left us—December.

Has left, like a friend that is true in the sun,
And false in the shadows.
He has found new delights, in the land where he's gone,
Greener woodlands and meadows.
What care we ? let him go ! let the snow shroud the lea,
Let it drift on the heather !
We can sing through it all ; I have you—you have me,
And we'll laugh at the weather.

The old year may die, and a new one be born
That is bleaker and colder ;
But it cannot dismay us ; we dare it—we scorn,
For love makes us bolder.
Ah Robin ! sing loud on the far-distant lea,
Thou friend in fair weather ;
But here is a song sung, that's fuller of glee,
By two warm hearts together.

1870.

THE TALE THE ROBIN TOLD.

I walked to-day, in the grassy dell,
  Where the cunning ground-bird hides her nest,
And just where the plum-tree's shadow fell,
  I sat me down for a while to rest.
And a robin came, and sat in the tree,
And told a long-lost tale to me.

Of a maiden, pure as the morning light,
  And fresh as a white rose, bathed in dew.
Of a youth with eyes like a stormy night,
  And a heart that nothing of candor knew.
And all through the valley, green and fair,
The youth and the maiden wandered there.

He plucked the violets, blue and pale,
  The lily white, and the roses red,
With every flower that decked the vale—
  But the maid was fairest of all, he said.
And the robin saw him kiss her cheek,
And the maiden blushed, but did not speak.

And he held her hand, in a lover's way,
  And he saw the blush that his glance awoke,
And with eye, and tone, he seemed to say
  The words that his false lips never spoke.

And of her strength, and her life a part,
Was the love that grew in the maiden's heart.

But the summer died, and the autumn came,
　　And the maiden walked in the vale alone ;
And the hopeless love, like a scorching flame,
　　Burned out her life, but she made no moan.
And she drooped, and died, as the year grew old,
And this was the tale that the robin told.

————

A MEMORY.

Oh, do you remember that night, long ago,
　　When I gave you the rose from my hair ?
And you whispered, " I'll wear it close over my heart,
　　As I cherish the sweet giver there ?"

'Twas a long time ago ? you've forgotten, perhaps,
　　That such a thing ever occurred.
But to-night, as I sit in the firelight's glow,
　　My heart's with the memory stirred,

And I seem to live over my girlhood again,
　　When my life was as warm as the spring :
Before it had read the sharp lesson of pain,
　　And when *you* were my hero, and king.

Oh! you were not worthy the love that I gave,
   Like the the sun in midsummer, it burned ;
While a passionless fancy, an idle day-dream,
   Was the poor, shallow thing you returned.

Long ago—long ago ! time has softened the pain,
   That threataned to shadow my life.
I am older, and wiser I think, now, than then,
   And you have a beautiful wife—

As pure as the angels, as fair, too, they say,
   With her blue eyes and snowy-white lid.
But I cannot help wondering, here to myself,
   If she loves you as well as I did.

Ah me ! it can never harm you, or your bride,
   For me to dream over that night,
When you whispered sweet words o'er the rose from
     my hair,
And my foolish heart throbbed in delight.

                    1868.

WAITING.

The days flow on, and on,
   And never one comes back.
Another year has vanished and gone,

As the waves of the sea wash out the track
 On the shining sands o' th' shore.
And patience waneth, and hope is spent,
As I wait and watch for the one who went,
 And cometh to me no more.

 The spring-time lived and died,
  And the summer followed fast;
And I watched through both, with a heart that cried,
For the one who vanished into the past,
 Like a beautiful star from the sky;
Who sailed in a good ship over the sea,
And the ship came back : "But where is he,
 Oh, treacherous ship," I cry ?

 The autumn, gold and brown,
  Rose from the summer's grave,
And the rain and my tears fell down and down,
As day by day I stood by the wave,
 And cried aloud in my pain.
But what cares the sea for a tortured soul !
It mocks at grief, and the breakers roll,
 Singing a loud refrain.

 And never a word from thee,
  But a silence deep as death;
Though the winter gleameth on moor and lea,
And the cold, cold wind, with its cruel breath,

Blows over the angry sea.
Yet alway and ever, till life is done,
Shall I watch, and wait, and weep for one
    Who cometh never, to me.

                1869.

DRIFTING APART.

Farther apart, each day, our lives are drifting;
    Farther apart at every set of sun.
The clouds between us show no signs of lifting,
    But droop, and gather shadows, one by one.

Drifting apart! the visions that I've cherished,
    Within my loving, foolish heart for years,
At those two meaning words, have rudely perished,
    And in their place is naught but bitter tears.

I do not weep—I do not sigh, and languish,
    And murmur at the hard decree of fate.
I walk my way, in silent, smiling anguish,
    Knowing remorse, and tears, are all too late.

But oh, my darling! I am only human,
    And though 'tis weakness, I do love you yet.
Mine is the heart, of clinging, constant woman,
    Whose lot it is to love, and not forget.

I know that we can never stem the current,
 That bore the sunshine of my life away;
Our feet can never cross the unbridged torrent
 That flows between us, wider every day.

Perhaps, when we have passed the heavenly portal,
 And all our tears are dried by Christ, the Friend,
And we have entered on the life immortal,
 Perhaps our path ways There may meet, and blend

I cannot tell ; the mystic, grand To-morrow
 Was never meant for earthly, mortal eyes.
But it is sweet, to think all tears and sorrow,
 Will vanish at the dawn of heavenly skies.

1868.

ONCE MORE TOGETHER.

[To II. A. M.]

What sounds so sweet as the glad words of greeting?
 And what starts the tears,
Like the warm kiss, that is given at meeting
 After long years.

Friend of my heart, we are once more together ;
 Hand clasped in hand.

We sit and we walk in the beautiful weather
    That gladdens the land.

Oh, rare golden days, in the heart of September ;
    Days more than sweet—
Days that my heart will forever remember,
    Ye are too fleet !

Why haste away ! the greedy " Past's " measure
    Already run's o'er ;
But like a miser who hoards up rare treasure,
    He cries out for " more."

Oh bright Autumn days ! If you only would linger
    And loiter, and stay !
Too soon old time shall be pointing his finger
    And bidding me say

That word "Good-bye," that's so hard to be spoken.
    Hearts have been stirred
Almost to breaking ; and fond hearts *have* broken
    At that last word.

Away with these sad thoughts! this rare golden weather
    Shall not find me sad,
Because we cannot *always* wander together,
    But I will be glad

Of the days that are left.   No foreboding of sorrow
  Shall darken my sky.
Nor To-day be o'erclouded, because some To-morrow.
  I must say good-bye.

1871.

ONCE IN A WHILE.

Once in a while, in this world so strange,
  To lighten our sad regrets,
We find a heart that is true through change—
  A heart that never forgets.
Oh rare as a blossoming rose in December—
  As a bird in an Arctic clime,
Is a heart, a *heart* that can remember
  Through sorrow and change and time.

Once in a while we find a love
  That will live through life and death,
Ay! that will follow the soul above,
  Not passing away with the breath.
But rarer, oh rarer by far and stranger
  Than a spring in the desert sand,
Is a love that will last, with toil, and danger,
  And strife on every hand.

Once in a while we find a friend
  That will cling through good or ill,

Whose friendship follows us e'en to the end,
   Be it up or adown the hill,
But the heart so true, and the love so tender,
   And friendship's faithful smile,
Whether we dwell in squalor or splendor,
   We find but "once in a while."

                  1872.

———

BEAUTY.

Though thy cheek be fair, as the roses are,
   Thy brow like the drifted snow,
And thine eye as bright, as the diamonds light,
   Yet if in thy heart doth grow
But noxious weeds, and selfish deeds
   Follow thy steps alway,
What in the end availeth it, friend,
   If thy face is fair, I pray.

For the smoothest brow, old Time will plow,
   And he dimmeth the brightest eye;
And the fairest face, and the form of grace,
   In the lowly grave must lie.
But our deeds live on, when life is done.
   Nor Time, nor death destroy ;
And the words we say, will make their way
   With sorrow, or with joy.

And even the thought, that we utter not,
  In heaven is like a shout.
And bad or good, it is understood,
  And the angels write it out.
But they do not care, if the face be fair,
  Or what the world deems plain.
They look to the heart, and the deathless part,
  For the rest is poor and vain.

1870.

A PLEA FOR FAME.

Let those slander fame who will—
  Call her cheat and blame her ways.
It may all be true ; and still
  I shall give her words of praise.
She has been my faithful friend,
  True and constant to the end.

Since I saw her hand first beckon
  Far above my lowly plain,
I have had no need to reckon
  What my loss, or what my gain.
She has made sweet blossoms blow
In whatever path I go ;
She hath made the dark ways light,
Made the somber places bright ;

She has filled my empty cup
   Full to overflow with pleasure,
And, though I may drink it up,
   She again refills the measure.

She has never promised aught
That she has not more than brought.
She has stood by me in danger,
Made a friend of many a stranger—
Made a welcome warm for me
Whereso'er my lot may be ;
Thrown wide open many a door
That was closed to me before ;
Given me every boon and blessing—
Almost—that is worth possessing.

All my life, I never knew
Any other friend so true.
Youth and Love are fleeting things ;
Wealth has light and airy wings—
Fame, once mine, will never flee,
She has been a friend to me.
Let who will condemn her ways.
I shall always sing her praise.

1872.

SOMEWHERE.

Somewhere there is a spot of ground,
  Covered with grass, or snow, may-be,
That one day will be spaded 'round
  And dug up to make room for me.

And I unconsciously have trod,
  Perhaps, and so again may tread
Upon the very voiceless sod,
  That will be roof above my head.

Somewhere upon the earth to-day
  Are dwelling men, who yet shall spade
And cut and dig the earth away,
  Until my narrow house is made.

Perchance they have clasped hands with me ;
  Those hands. that, after I am dead,
Shall measure me so reverently,
  To find how long to make my bed.

How strangely, solemn thoughts like these
  Will come, when life seems blithe and gay;
Like voices of the passing breeze,
  Saying "All things must pass away-"

OUR ANGEL.

Upon a couch all robed by careful hands
  For her repose, the maiden Mable lies,
Her long bright hair is braided in smooth bands—
  A mass of stranded gold, that mortal eyes

May, wondering, gaze upon a little while ;
  That mortal hands may touch a few times more.
Her placid lips part in a sweet, faint smile,
  As if the glories of that mystic shore,

When first they fell upon her spirit eyes—
  All the rare splendors of that unseen way
Had touched her with a wondering, glad surprise,
  And left the pleased expression on her clay.

Her two fair hands are crossed upon her breast—
  Two shapes of wax upon a drift of snow.
And they have robed her for her peaceful rest,
  Not in the hateful shroud—that sign of woe,

But in that garb we loved to see her wear ;
  A dark blue robe, fashioned by her own hand.
I wonder, as I see her lying there,
  If God will give her spirit in His land

8

Another shape.   She could not be more fair.
　I think he will not change her form, or face,
But with the same long, rippling, golden hair
　She will kneel down before the throne of grace,

And wipe God's feet ; and her dark eyes will raise
　Up to Christ's face, and touch Him with her hand,
And will with her own sweet voice, sing God's praise,
　And still be fairest in the Angel band.

1872.

A SUMMER IDYL.

I hear the sound of the reapers,
　All in the golden grain,
And voices of strong young binders,
　Singing a sweet refrain.
The winds are asleep on the hilltops,
　And the sun smiles down in the vale,
Till the rose faints under his glances,
　And her cheek grows wan and pale.

The meadows are green as the ocean ;
　And the winds, when they wake from rest,
Ripple and billow the grasses,
　Like waves on the ocean's breast.
The vine grows over my window,

Where the humming bird comes each day,
And the robin and thrush in the willow,
   Are singing their lives away.

Oh beautiful, languid Summer !
   You are so fleet, so fleet.
Oh youth, and joy, and gladness,
   You are so sweet—so sweet !
My life is a wonderful poem,
   Complete in measure and rhyme,
And the sweetest of all the stanzas
   Is written this summer time.

But the golden harvest is going—
   The summer will fade and pass.
The thrush and the robin will vanish,
   And the snow fall over the grass.
The vine at my window will perish,
   And the beautiful poem of life
Will change to a measure of sorrow,
   And be marred and broken by strife.
Then revel in youth, and summer ;
   Oh heart, be glad and gay,
For sorrow, and blight, and winter,
   Are coming to us one day.

1872.

THE MUSICIANS.

The strings of my heart were strung by Pleasure,
   And I laughed, when the music fell on my ear,
For he and Mirth played a joyful measure,
   And they played so loud that I could not hear
The wailing and moaning of souls a-weary—
   The strains of sorrow that floated around,
For my heart's notes rang loud and cheery,
   And I heard no other sound.

Mirth and Pleasure, the music brothers,
   Played louder and louder in joyful glee;
But sometimes a discord was heard by others—
   Though only the rythm was heard by me.
Louder and louder, and faster and faster
   The hands of the brothers played strain on strain,
When all of a sudden a Mighty Master
   Swept them aside ; and Pain,

Pain, the musician, the soul-refiner,
   Restrung the strings of my quivering heart,
And the air that he played was a plaintive minor,
   So sad that the tear-drops were forced to start ;
Each note was an echo of awful anguish,
   As shrill as solemn, as sharp as slow,
And my soul for a season seemed to languish
   And faint with its weight of woe.

With skillful hands, that were never weary,
   This Master of Music played strain on strain,
And between the bars of the miserere,
   He drew up the strings of my heart again :
And I was filled with a vague, strange wonder,
   To see that they did not snap in two.
"They are drawn so tight they will break asunder,"
   I thought, but instead, they grew,

In the hands of the Master, firmer and stronger;
   And I could hear on the stilly air—
Now my ears were deafened by Mirth no longer—
   The sounds of sorrow, and grief, and despair,
And my soul grew tender and kind to others ;
   My nature grew sweeter, my mind grew broad ;
And I held all men to be my brothers,
   Linked by the chastening rod.

My soul was lifted to God and heaven,
   And when on my heart-strings fell again
The hands of Mirth and Pleasure, even,
   There was never a discord to mar the strain.
For Pain, the musician, the soul-refiner,
   Attuned the strings with a Master hand,
And whether the music be major or minor,
   It is always sweet and grand.

                 1872.

IN VAIN.

The artist looks down on his canvass,
   And smothers a heart-weary sigh,
And he sees not the beautiful picture
   That glows with the hues of the sky.
For a picture that cannot be painted
   Burns into the artist's brain,
And he weeps as he sits at his easel,
   And sobs through his sorrow, " In vain."

The poet reads over his poem,
   The thoughts of a Heaven-lent soul—
And sweet as the ripple of waters
   The beautiful sentences roll.
But a poem that cannot be written,
   Burns into the poet's brain,
And he weeps in a passion of anguish,
   And sobs through his sorrow, " In vain."

The musician sits at his organ,
   And the air echoes sweet melodies.
But his heart cries for sounds that are better
   Than the sounds that he draws from the keys.
For a chord that has never been sounded—
   A passionate,—ecstatic strain.
And he weeps as he sits at the organ,   .
   And sobs through his sorrow, " In vain."

Oh Artist, Musician and Poet !
   Three souls that were lent to the earth
To brighten with fingers of beauty
   This bare, barren planet of dearth !
You dream of the glories of Heaven,
   And vainly are striving to show
To the gaze of the clay-fettered mortals,
   The things that no mortal shall know.

1871.

BABY EVA.

[Lines to the sweetest little girl in the world.]

Sitting and watching the fire-light fall
In fitful gleams, on floor, and wall,
I think of the fairest of baby-girls,
With bright blue eyes, and sunny curls,
With two round cheeks, and a dimpled hand—
The sweetest baby in all the land.

I think of her thousand coaxing arts,
That won her place in my heart of hearts ;
And how at twilight, the baby's hour—
A winsome queen, she ruled in power ;
And laid on my shoulder her head of gold
And named the stories she wanted told.

" Goosey Loosey," " Cat and Mouse,"
" London Bridge," and " Jack and his House,"
" Peter's Pig," and " the Foolish Frog,"
" The Mooley Cow," and " the Poly-wog."
And when these were told, as many more,
Till I needs must add, to my ample atore.

I can think how the bright little eyes would glow
At the tale of the kid that was made to go.
How they filled with tears, when Old Mother Hubbard
Opened the door on an empty cupboard.
How they sparkled with glee, and glowed with fun
When she heard how the wasp made the hornet run.

Over and over the winsome elf
Would plead for the stories she knew herself;
She would sigh o'er the fate of poor Hen-Pen
Who foolishly hid in the Fox's den,
And grieve o'er the poor little mouse that was drowned
Before his " great long tail " was found.

And sitting alone in the fire-light's glow,
And thinking about it, all I know
That not on the earth, in any place,
Is there such another winsome face—
Is there another, so sweet and wise,
As baby Eva—beneath the skies.

1873.

I SHALL NOT FORGET.

I shall not forget you.   The years may be tender,
  But vain are their efforts to soften my smart ;
And the strong hands of Time are too feeble and slender
  To garland the grave that is made in my heart.
Your image is ever about me—before me,
  Your voice floats abroad on the voice of the wind ;
And the spell of your presence, in absence, is o'er me,
  And the dead of the past, in the present I find.

I cannot forget you.   The one boon ungiven,
  The boon of your love, is the cross that I bear.
In the midnight of sorrow I vainly have striven
  To crush in my heart the sweet image hid there ;
To banish the beautiful dreams that are thronging
  The halls of my memory—dreams worse than vain ;
For the one drop withheld, I am thirsting and longing,
  For the one joy denied, I am weeping in pain.

I would not forget you.   I live to remember
  The beautiful hopes that bloomed but to decay,
And brighter than June glows the bleakest December,
  When peopled with ghosts of the dreams passed away.
Once loving you truly, I love you forever ;
  I mourn not in weak, idle grief for the past ;
But the love in my bosom can never, oh never
  Pass out, or another pass in, first or last.

THE OLD AND THE NEW.

As a mother who dies in travail—
   Who closes her eyes in death,
And sinks in the sleep that is long and deep,
   With her babe's first wailing breath,
In the hush of the midnight watches,
   So the old year passed away,
And the new was born, and was hailed this morn,
   As the " Happy New Year Day."

The day when our eyes look backward,
   To see what our hands have done,
Through the hours of gold that the dead year told,
   Like the beads of a pious Nun—
When we shut up the blotted ledger,
   With its record of joy and grief,
Of losses and gains, and pleasures and pains,
   And turn to the new white leaf.

We hoped, we planned, and we promised,
   When the year that is dead was young :
But our hopes are like leaves that are withered,
   And the year like a song that is sung.
We planned out some wonderful project,
   That should bring to us riches and fame :
Hour by hour, day by day, our plans fell away,
   And our project was only a name.

We promised that life should be better,
 As the sphere of our labors grew broad,
That "those things behind" should pass from the mind,
 As we reached for the prize of our God.
But alas, for the promises given !
 Lo, what were our good resolves worth ?
They were lost to our sight, and we strayed from the
  light,
 And worshiped the poor things of earth.

And so while we builded our castles,
 Wirh turrets of sapphire and gold,
Till they glowed in the sun, the months one by one,
 Slipped away, and the year grew old—
Grew feeble and old and departed
 In the shadows and gloom of the night ;
And some said 'twas a year full of sorrow,
 And some, 'twas a year of delight.

Some, sitting in darkness and weeping,
 Sob, " Oh, but the year was so long !"
And some, full of cheer, say the beautiful year
 Was only one verse of a song.
To some it brought gladness and pleasure,
 To others but sorrow and gloom.
It gave one the sweet orange blossoms,
 Another, the dust of the tomb.

There are mothers to-day who are sitting,
   With arms that are aching to hold
The small form of grace, and the dear little face,
   And the head with its crown of spun gold ;
And they think of the last happy New Year,
   And the voice that made music all day,
And, sitting alone in the silence, they moan,
   For the babe that is hidden away.

There are maidens, in love-letters, reading
   The story so old and so new ;
And their happy hearts beat, in a rythm so sweet,
   As they read of the love strong and true ;
And they think that of all the glad New Years,
   There was never another so glad ;
And they heed not the wail of the mother, so pale,
   Who thinks the day dreary and sad.

There are some leaning over the coffin
   Of a hope that went out with the year ;
And their sad eyes are dry, and the lips white that cry,
   " The hope of a life-time lies here."
God pity and comfort such mourners,
   For God alone knoweth the pain
Of these suffering hearts, when a dear hope departs,
   And is buried to rise not again.

It is sad to lean over a lov'd one,
   And cover the face with a pall,

But who mourns, with bowed head, o'er a hope that is
    dead,
  Has the bitterest sorrow of all.
God grant that this New Year may bring them,
  Some other hope, fully as sweet ;
May it cull the bright flowers from happiness' bowers,
  And cast them in wreaths at their feet.

Despair and delight walk together ;
  The sunshine falls over the tomb ;
And close by the weary, whose lives are all dreary,
  Walk those who are crowned with earth's bloom.
Some wearing the laurels of glory,
  And flushed with the glow of success,
May their wreaths never pale, or their honors grow stale,
  Or their hopes or their happiness less.

Oh wonderful year that has left us !
  Full of tragedy, sorrow and change,
Was there ever another so fateful,
  Was there ever another so strange ?
Great hearts that were throbbing last New Year
  Are food for the grave-worms to-day,
And lips whose least word a whole nation heard,
  Are nothing but cold, silent clay.

There was one who was crowned with the Fern Leaves,
  Whose ringing tones, full of good cheer,

Lightened hearts that were sad, and made weary ones
    glad,
  On many a weary New Year.
There was one double-dowered by heaven,
    Twice gifted and favored by God,
REID, whose brush, and whose pen, made him king
    among men,—
  He, too, lieth under the sod.

And another, the hero of battles,
  Before whom the enemy fled
In alarm and dismay, while he won the day,
  MEAD,—warrior and hero, is dead.
There was one who climbed up the steep ladder,
  Step by step, on rounds that he made ;
And carved out his name, on the summit of Fame,
  In letters that never will fade.

He struggled for knowledge and riches,
  Position and and glory, and *won*.
But, reaching too far, like a child for a star,
  He fell, with the words, " It is done !"
It is done, all the climbing and toiling ;
  It is done, all the worry and strife,
All the bitter and sweet, th' success and defeat,—
  It is done, the great drama of life.

It is done, all the year could do for us,
  Its mixture of shadow and sun,

Its smiles and its tears, its hopes and its fears,
   Its labors and duties, all done.
We stand face to face with the New Year,
   Nor know what it hides from our sight ;
God grant that it be kind to you, and to me,
   That it lead us in ways that are light.

The bells in the steeples are joyful,
   The children are shouting in glee,
There is mirth and good cheer in the happy New Year—
   All hail to young '73 !
Come out of the shadows, ye mourners !
   And drop, for this one day at least,
Your mantles of woe, and let us all go
   And take part in the revel and feast.

Let us laugh like gay children together,
   Forgetting we ever shed tears—
Forgetting the losses, the sorrows and crosses
   That came to our lives with the years—
Remembering only the perfume,
   The beauty, the bloom, and the sun,
Let us talk of the New Years departed,
   And call this the happiest one.

                January 1st, 1873.

DECORATION POEM.

A year that was solemn, and sad and strange,
  Has passed away to its tomb,
Since we made the graves of our dear, dead braves
  Like a garden, all abloom,—
A year that brought sorrow, and want, and change—
  A year with a fateful breath :
And the dreaded beat of its flame-shod feet
  Wrought ruin, and woe, and death.

High and higher the tongues of fire
  Leaped up in a single night,
Till the walls of a town went crumbling down,
  And a city fell in her might.
And with flame and disease, and woes like these,
  Death laughed in his mad, wild glee ;
And Pestilence loosened his imps in the land,
  And ships went down at sea.

But with all of the passion, and pain, and fear,—
  With all of the long, sad hours,—
We have not forgotten to offer here
  Our yearly tribute of flowers.
I think the heart in a loyal breast
  Knows no such word as *forget ;*
And I think—nay, know—that in weal or in woe,
  We shall remember our debt.

The debt of a nation redeemed from shame,
   And a million of slaves set free,
Of a spotless fame, and cherished name,
   Honored on land and sea.
Of the dear old flag kept out of the dust,
   The flag of the brave and true,
And this is the debt we are owing yet
   To the boys who wore the blue.

Thousands are sleeping in Southern graves,
   With no slab to tell us where ;
But the land where the sweet magnolia waves,
   God's hands keep fresh and fair.
And the angels above; in pity and love,
   Watch over the unknown mound,
Where some heart's joy, some mother's boy,
   A nameless grave has found.

To a clear sweet song that is free and strong,
   Yet sad with a minor strain,
I liken the lives of the boys in blue,
   Who died ere they knew our gain ;
To a glad, glad song, that rings loud and bold,
   In a stirring major key,
I liken in thought, the boys who fought,
   And were crowned with victory.

To the hero who comes with the beating of drums,
   We can give the laurels of fame ;

And with mirth, and music, and song and feast,
　　We can honor and praise his name ;
But we bring to the bed of the sainted dead,
　　Only these wreaths to-day ;
Yet they speak with their bloom and sweet perfume,
　　More than our lips can say.

They speak of a love that can never die,
　　But strengthen and grow with time ;
Of lives that blossom again on high,—
　　Of a faith and hope sublime.
They tell how a grateful nation's heart
　　Remembers her tried and true,
And how tears are shed for the honored dead,
　　For the boys who wore the blue.

They speak of the higher and purer life
　　That the Lord's dear angels know ;
Where nought can enter of pain or strife,
　　And tears can never flow.
Sleep on brave boys your graves are as green
　　As the thoughts we give to ye,
And these blooms will say ye are shrined alway
　　In the halls of memory.

　　　　　　FOREST HILL CEMETERY, May 30th, 1872.

AT SET OF SUN.

If we sit down at set of sun,
And count the things that we have done,
    And counting, find
One self-denying act, one word
That eased the heart of him who heard,
    One glance, most kind,
That fell like sunshine where it went—
Then we may count that day well spent.

Or, on the other hand, if we,
In looking through the day, can see
    A place or spot
Where we an unkind act put down,
Or where we smiled when wont to frown,
    Or crushed some thought
That cumbered the heart—ground where it stood—
Then we may count that day as good.

But if, through all the life-long day,
We've eased no heart by yea or nay ;
    If through it all
We've done no thing that we can trace,
That brought the sunshine to a face—
    No act most small
That helped some soul, and nothing cost—
Then count that day as worse than lost.

1869.

LOVE SONG.

When the glad spring time walked over the border,
   And the brown honey bee crept from his cell;
When the sun and the west wind put nature in order,
   And decked her in robes that became her so well,
Then did my torpid heart waken from slumber,
   Then did I first spring to life and to light.
For what were the years passed without thee; they number
   Only as one long, dark, flavorless night.

In the flush of the spring time, I saw thee, and seeing,
   Loved with the love that had waited for thee.
A life that I never had known, sprang to being—
   A life and a love that were heaven to me.   .
There never before was such warmth in the summer,
   There never before were such hues in the fall,
Never such balm in the breath of that comer
   Who shrouds the dead seasons, and rules over all.

Love, I have drank in the charm of thy presence,
   The elixir that grants me perpetual life.
My blood leaps, and bounds! I am thrilled with the
      essence,
   And soar over trials, and troubles, and strife.
We live, and we love! and what grief can alarm us;
   Darling, my darling, the world is our own!

Life never can rob us—death cannot disarm us
  Of this, our vast riches, our wealth, love, alone.

The summer is dead ! did'st know it, my darling ?
  Did'st know that the winter walked over the earth ?
The gold-breasted thrush, and the quaker-crowned starling
  Make glad other lands, with their innocent mirth.
Ah no ! for the summer of love in thy bosom,
  Make summer and sunlight, for thee, everywhere.
I should not have known : but I missed the bright
     blossom
That all through the summer, I saw in thy hair.

               1870.

DISPLAY.

Oh households wherein skeletons abide !
  Keep the dark closet closed, nor think it wise
  To throw the door open for stranger eyes,
To see the grinning, fleshless thing inside.

I hate that senseless, imbecile display
  Of loathsome things, that calls the gaping crowd
  To gaze and comment.   Let the screening shroud
Cover the faces of the dead, I say.

And if a household counts a skeleton,
  Then keep the ghastly phantom closeted ;

Nor flaunt the bones of the unquiet dead
For all the vulgar throng to gaze upon.

Oh you whose souls are burdened cruelly,
   Who shrink in anguish at the bitter smart
   That gnaweth, burneth, at your very heart—
Cover the wounds, that strangers shall not see !

Think you a bleeding heart will sooner heal,
   To hang where all the cutting winds that blow,
   And all the birds of prey can mock its woe ?
I hate that vain parade, of all we feel.

Whoever knew the world to give relief
   To any private sorrow of a heart !
   Its sneering pity is a poisoned dart !
Then closet well your phantoms, and your grief.

1869.

AT THE WINDOW.

Every morning, as I walk down
From my dreary lodgings, toward the town,
I see at the window near the street,
The face of a woman, fair, and sweet,
With soft brown eyes, and chestnut hair,
And red lips, warm with the kiss left there.

And she lingers as long as she can see
The man who walks, just ahead of me.

At night, when I come from my office, down town,
There stands the woman, with eyes of brown,
Smiling out through the window-blind,
At the man who comes strolling on behind.
This fellow and I resemble each other ;
At least, so I'm told, by one and another.
(But I think I'm the handsomer, far, of the two.)
I don't know him at all, save to " how d'ye do,"
Or nod when I meet him.   I think he's at work
In a dry goods store, as a salaried clerk.

And I am a lawyer, of high renown ;
Have a snug bank account, and an office down town.
Yet I feel for that fellow an envious spite :
(It has no better name, so I speak it outright.)
There were symptoms before: but it's grown, I believe,
Alarmingly fast, since one cloudy eve,
When passing the little house, close by the street,
I heard the patter of two tiny feet,
And a figure in pink, fluttered down to the gate,
And a sweet voice exclaimed, "Oh, Will, you are late
And, darling, I've watched at the window until——
Sir, I beg pardon ! I thought it was Will."

I passed on my way, with an odd little smart
  Beneath my vest pocket, in what's called the heart.

For, as it happens, *my* name, too, is Will ;
And that voice crying "darling" sent such a strange thrill
Throughout my whole being. "How nice it would be,"
Thought I, " if it were in reality me
That she's watched and longed for, instead of that lout."
(It was *envy* made me use that word, no doubt,
For he's a fine fellow, and handsome, ahem !)
But then it's absurd that this rare little gem
Of a woman, should be on the look-out for him,
Till she brings on a headache, and makes her eyes dim,
While I go to lodgings, dull, dreary, and bare,
With no one to welcome me, no one to care
If I'm early, or late—no soft eyes of brown
To watch when I go to, or come from, the town.

This bleak, wretched bachelor life, is about,
If I may be allowed the expression—played out.
Somewhere there must be, in this wide world, I think,
Another fair woman, who dresses in pink.
And I know of a cottage for sale just below,
And it has a French window, in front, and—heigho
I wonder how long, at the longest, 'twill be,
Before coming home from the office I'll see
A nice little woman there, watching for me.

1870.

HOW.

How can I let my youth go by?
  How can I let Time mark my brow,
And steal the light of a laughing eye,
  And whiten the locks that are nut brown now.
      And the tide that goes,
      And ripples, and flows,
Like a beautiful river, on forever,
Over my head, through every vein,
And fills me, and thrills me, with joy like pain,
      Old cruel Time,
      With a touch of rime,
Will drug, and chill, and freeze, until
      It likes a stream,
      In its winter dream.

Ho! ho! old Time! you may chuckle and smile,
  But *Death* may cheat you, and beat you yet;
What shall you say, if, after a while,
  Ere the sun of my youth has set,
I go with him, to a closet dim,
  And closing my eyes, in a long, long rest,
      Lie white and cold,
      And never grow old,
  With my two hands clasped over my breast.

Always young,
     With my song half sung—
Lying under the graves' green mould ;
          And the world, for a day
          Would miss me, and say,
" When will the rest of the tale be told ?"
          And then go on,
          Gaily on,
Till its hopes were fears, and its young were old.

          And, lying there,
          What should I care,
Though Time, in a phrenzy of baffled rage,
          Should beat on my grave,
          And howl and rave,
That I would not barter my youth, for age ;
          But lie and sleep,
          Down low and deep,
Though suns of a thousand seasons set.
          Always young,
               Never old,
          With my song half sung,
               And my tale half told—
Ho, ho, old Time, I may cheat you yet !

                              December, 1869.

BY AND BY.

Sometime fame shall come to me ;
Sometime in the " yet to be."
Not to-day, and not to-morrow;
After years of toil and sorrow,
After loosing youth and grace,
In the weary, foolish chase,

After weeks of bitter tears,
After months, and after years,
After waiting day on day,
Throwing love, and peace away,
I shall find the phantom nearing—
I shall find the shadows clearing.

I shall reach the thing I sought,
I shall reach, and find it—what ?
Will it recompense, and pay
For the joys I cast away ?
In the weary, weary race,
When I lost my youth, and grace ?

Is it worth the wear, and strife—
Worth the best part of a life ?
Thus have men and women queried,
Standing on the summit, wearied

With the long and steep ascent,
When their youth and grace were spent.

Time sweeps onward with his cycle :
Life is brief, and love is fickle.
I will pause not at his calling,
I will heed not tear-drops falling:
Fame, but Fame, will satisfy,
I shall find it by and by.

1870.

KING AND SIREN.

The harsh king, Winter, sat upon the hills,
    And reigned, and ruled the earth right royally.
He locked the rivers, lakes, and all the rills.
    "I am no puny, maudlin king," quoth he,
But a stern monarch, born to rule and reign,
    And I will show my power to the end ;
The summer's flowery retinue I've slain.
    And taken the bold, free North-Wind for my friend.

Spring, Summer, Autumn—feeble queens they were,
    With their vast troops of flowers, birds, and bees,
And winds, that made the long, green grasses stir—
    They lost their own identity in these.
I scorn them all ! nay, I defy them all !

And none can wrest the sceptre from my hand.
The trusty North-Wind answers to my call,
  And breathes his icy breath upon the land."

The Siren, South-Wind, listening the while.
  Now floated airily across the lea.
" Oh, King !" she said, with tender tone and smile,
  " I come to do all homage unto thee.
In all the sunny region whence I came,
  I find none like thee, King, so brave and grand.
Thine is a well-deserved, unrivalled fame ;
  I kiss in awe, dear King, thy cold white hand."

Her words were pleasing, and most fair her face.
  He listened wrapt, to her soft-whispered praise.
She nestled nearer, in her Siren grace ;
    "Dear King," she said, "henceforth my voice shall
       raise
But songs of thy unrivalled splendor l Lo !
  How white thy brow is! How thy garments shine—
I tremble 'neath thy beaming glance, for oh,
  Thy wondrous beauty mak'st thee seem divine."

The vain king listened, in a trance of bliss,
  To this most sweet sweet voiced Siren from the south.
She nestled close, and pressed a lingering kiss
  Upon the stern white pallor of his mouth.
She hung upon his breast—she pressed his cheek—

And he was nothing loth to hold her there.
While she such tender, loving words did speak
    And combed his white locks, with her fingers fair.

And so she bound him, in her Siren wiles,
    And stole his strength with every glance she gave,
And stabbed him through and through with tender smiles,
    And with her loving words she dug his grave.
And then she left him : old, and weak, and blind—
    And unlocked all the rivers, lakes and rills,
While the Queen Spring, with her whole troop behind,
    Of flowers, and birds, and bees, came over the hills.

                                    1871.

AFTER ?

After the summer glory has departed,
    After the sun slides low adown the skies,
After each snowy rose, and the red-hearted,
    Droops in the chilling blast, and faints, and dies,
When the brown bee no longer seeks the clover,
    But flies away, and hides in his honeyed den,
And from the bleak hills cutting winds blow over,
    Full of keen darts—ah, will you love me then ?

Or is it but the passion heat of Summer,
    That you mistake for love within your heart ?
And will not Winter, that unwelcome comer,

With his cold, scornful sneers, make it depart ?
Have not the subtle odors of the flowers
   Drugged you, and made you drunk with rare perfumes?
And when the winter crashes through the bowers,
   Will not your love fade, with the fading blooms ?

If so, I will not listen to your wooing ;
   And I will turn from words and glances sweet.
Because I will not hear a drunkard's sueing—
   Drunken with rose-scents, and the summer heat.
But if you woo me, in sound mind, and reason,
   And can convince me fully it is so,
And that your love will last through any season,
   Why then, my answer will not *quite* be—No.

                    1870.

IF YOU HAD BEEN TRUE.

Love, in the glow of the sunset,
   I have been thinking of you.
Thinking what you might have made me,
   If you had been constant and true.
You know I built wonderful castles,
   And you had a part in them all ;
But you cheated me, Love, you remember,
   And down fell each beautiful wall.

Well, you see I lost faith in all women—
    The very worst thing I could do.
Thought they were all of one pattern,
    And that was inconstant, untrue.
I know it was but a mad fancy:
    Know women are truer than men.
But I wish I had found it out sooner,
    Or could live my life over again.

For you see I have wasted my manhood;
    I don't really care to tell how.
And if I could live it all over,
    I think I could better it now.
I would marry some nice little woman—
    Some other, if I couldn't get you.
And I would be tender and faithful,
    And she would be constant and true.

                1870.

AFLOAT.

Once there was a boat, locked fast to a shore,
    But rust ate the chain, day by day,
And the boat was loosened more and more,
    As the fastenings slipped away.
Yet, any day, an outstretched hand,
Could have caught, and locked it again to land.

But never a hand was stretched to save,
  And the boat at last was free ;
And shot like an arrow over the wave,
  And drifted out mid-sea.
And never, oh never, across the main,
Will the boat to the shore be brought again.

So was my heart, love—linked to thine ;
  But neglect ate the chains away :
Yet a tender word love, I opine,
  Would have saved it, any day.
Ay ! a tender word, said first or last,
Would have mended the chain, and held it fast.

But the word was lacking : and so my heart,
  Slipped from its chains, like the boat.
And then as the last link fell apart,
  It sped o'er the waves—afloat.
Nor pleading hands, nor words, you see,
Brings the boat to shore, or my heart to thee.

ROSES AND LILIES.

Roses and Lilies, both are sweet ;
  Lily and Rose, both are fair;
But which to gather for mine alway,
  Which to gather, and keep, and wear,

10

That is the queston that bothers me,
For I cannot wear them both, you see.

Rose is the brightest and blithest of girls :
    I could lay my heart at her tiny feet,
And gaze forever in those dark eyes,
    And kiss forever those lips so sweet.
And holding her soft, white, clinging hand,
Dreamily float into Eden land.

And Lily—Lily, my ocean pearl,
    So sweetly tender, so moonlight fair,
I could float to heaven upon her smile,
    And kiss forever her silken hair,
That droppeth down, like a golden veil
Over her cheek, and brow—snow pale.

Lilies and Roses—both are fair :
    Rose, or Lily, which shall it be ?
I love them both with my heart of hearts,
    But I cannot wed them both, you see.
Dark-eyed Rose, my winsome girl—
    Moon-faced Lily, my ocean pearl.

                                        1870.

IN HEAVEN WITH YOU.

'Tis said, when we shall go across the river,
　　Whose bridge is death, and gain the other side,
There in that land, with God, the mighty Giver,
　　The heart shall evermore be satisfied.

And yet, sometimes I cannot help but wonder,
　　How I can live in heaven without your love ;
How live, rejoicing, through all time, I ponder,
　　And not have *you*, even with God above.

We bear such things on earth, for we remember
　　That life is but a little span, at best.
Its passion summer, but precedes December,
　　And in the grave, we say, there will be rest.

But after death, time stretches with no limit :
　　Your love, no time can ever bring to me.
Is heaven so bright this shadow can not dim it ?
　　It seems so long—that strange Eternity.

　　How could my heart, and soul, change so completely
　　　　That I should never think of this up there ?
　　But in the angel choruses join sweetly,
　　　　Nor ever feel this gnawing grief, and care.

How vast God's lore! how vain the skill of mortal!
    He did not mean that we should understand,
Until our feet had crossed the shining portal,
    The things so deep, and fathomless, and grand.

And He has made a heaven—a place most holy,
    For His redeemed to sometime enter in.
And there is room for all the meek and lowly,
    Whose faith, through sorrow hath washed out all sin.

And I believe, when we shall cross the river,
    Whose bridge is death, and reach the other side,
There in that land, with God the gracious Giver,
    Our hearts shall evermore be satisfied.

                                        1869.

THOU DOST NOT KNOW.

Thou dost not know it ! but to hear
    One word of praise from thee,
There is no pain I would not bear—
    No task too great for me.
My hands could tireless toil all day,
    My feet could tireless run,
If at the close thy lips would say,
    " Brave, noble heart, well done."

Thou dost not know it ! but to win
   Approval from thine eyes,
My soul has conquered many a sin,
   And conquering. neared tee skies.
And though the reward may not be given,
   In all my earthly days,   .
I feel that after death—in heaven,
   Thy lips will give me praise.

Thou dost not know—may never know,
   That all I strive to be,
All things praiseworthy that I do,
   I strive, and do, for thee.
And though I seldom see thy face,
   Or touch thy hand, my friend,
Those meetings are the means of grace,
   That help me to the end.

Thou dost not know that thy grand life
   Has been my beacon light.
I aim to conquer in the strife,
   That I may reach thy height.
I strive to live, so that my feet
   May walk the fields most fair,
For the after-life, seems, oh ! so sweet,
   Because *thou* wilt be there.

Thou dost not know how brave and strong
   A woman's heart can be.

But few could hide so well and long
   What mine has hid from thee.
So well, that should this idyl chance
   To meet thine eye, my friend,
Thou'd scan it with a careless glance,
   Nor dream to whom 'twas penned.

1872.

A GOLDEN YEAR.

Linger, linger, oh royal year !
   For I grieve to see you dying.
Rest on the hilltops—loiter near ;
   Wait, O Time, in your flying.
For never, in all the twice ten years,
   You have brought to build my twenty,
Never was one so free from tears—
   So overflowing with plenty.

Filled to the brim with the purest draughts,
   That I sip in fearless pleasure ;
While an unseen spirit watches and laughs,
   And again refills the measure.
My brightest dreams, and my fondest hopes,
   The year has gathered together,
And right bountifully they have come to me,
   From the Spring to the Autumn weather.

The rarest of flowers, subtle and sweet,
    That grew in the world Ideal,
Have dropped their seeds in the soil at my feet,
    And blossomed among the Real.
And Love, like a rose, still blossoms and blows,
    Passion-hearted, yet tender.
And my path is strewn with the glories of June,
    And I'm hedged about with its splendor.

Care flew over the hills, one day,
    And I sang, as he swift retreated;
And Hope took his crown, and Joy settled down,
    On the throne where Care had been seated.
Contentment hedged me all round about,
    And Love built his blazing fire;
And Happiness poured his treasures out,
    And left me with no desire.

I have walked breast high in a sea of bliss:
    I have loved my God, and my brother.
There never before was a year like this—
    There never can be another.
Linger, loiter, a little while,
    For I grieve to see you dying!
But even in grief, I can only smile,
    For my heart is too light for sighing.

                                    December, 1870.

FORESHADOWED.

My life has been a summer day complete,
Teeming with pleascres, tender, pure, and sweet.
But tiny clouds have ever dimmed the sky,
And they have quickly passed, and floated by.

Oh, seldom in this thorny world of ours,
Is mortal's pathway so bestrewn with flowers.
Fragrant and fair, they ever blow and bloom,
Untouched by chilling frosts, and wintry gloom.
And I thank God, for all his tenderness,
And from my very soul adore, and bless
Him who has cast my lines in pleasant ways,
And crowned with joy and happiness my days.

But sometimes, though the sun shines clear and bright,
And all the world seems full of joy and light,
A nameless shadow, none but I can see,
Falls on my heart, hushing its melody.
A nameless, voiceless shadow ; but I know
It tells of future agony and woe.
Some mighty sorrow, vague and undefined,
But dark, and awful, waits for me, behind
That shadowy cloud.' Something of woe and tears—
Of grief, and anguish, is the future years.

It floats away, and I rejoice again,
With all my warm young heart untouched by pain.
But ever and anon I see it loom,
Over my life, and feel its awful gloom.

Oh God ! I know not what is hidden there.
But give me strength to suffer and to bear.
Oh guide my soul ! and teach me how to pray,
And make my spirit stronger every day.
Upon Thy mighty arm, oh ! let me rest,
And lean.   And when Thou deemest best,
Reveal, my Father, what is hid behind
The nameless shadow, vague, and undefined.

1869.

FORTUNE'S WHEEL.

My Love was a poor man's daughter,
  And I was a poor man's son.
And oft we walked on the sea shore,
  When the work of the day was done.
Hand in hand, on the gleaming strand,
  And our two hearts beat as one.

My Love was meek, and gentle,
  And she was wondrous fair ;
With hazel dyes in her slumbrous eyes,

And chestnut shades in her hair.
And we raked hay on the meadow,
   And I gave my heart in her care.

But the great, notched wheel of Fortune,
   Kept turning on and on.
And she was a rich man's daughter,
   And I was a poor man's son.
And she had a score of lovers, or more.
   But I was the favored one.

And I passed hard by her window,
   Nor turned my face to see
The lady fair, with gems in her hair,
   As fine as fine could be.
Though I knew her heart was dying
   For just one word from me.

My Love grew pale as the lily,
   And faded day by day,
And I passed by, and heard her sigh,
   And turned my face away.
For I was proud as the proudest—
   And her gold between us lay.

And the great, notched wheel of Fortune
   Kept rolling on and on.
   And she was a poor man's daughter,

And I was a rich man's son.
And maids of grace smiled in my face,
But I saw only one.

I found my love in the cottage,
Where first I sought her side.
And I shall not tell *how* I wooed—but well,
For she had not my pride.
And I gave my heart in her keeping,
And won her for my bride.

1870.

SEARCHING.

These quiet autumn days,
My soul, like Noah's dove, on airy wings
Goes out, and searches for the hidden things,
Beyond the hills of haze.

With mournful, pleading cries
Above the waters of the voiceless sea
That laps the shores of broad Eternity.
Day after day it flies.

Searching, but all in vain,
For some stray leaf that it may light upon,
And read the future as the days agone—
Its pleasure and its pain.

Listening, patiently,
For some voice speaking from the mighty deep,
Revealing all the secrets it doth keep,
  In silence, there for me.

  Come back and wait! my soul,
Day after day thy search has been in vain,
Voiceless and silent o'er the future's plain
  Its mystic waters roll.

  God seeing, knoweth best,
And in his time the waters shall subside,
And thou shalt know what lies beneath the tide.
  Then wait, my soul, and rest.

1869.

DAFT.

In the warm yellow smile of the morning,
  She stands at the lattice pane,
And watches the strong young binders
  Stride down to the fields of grain ;
And she counts the over and over
  As they pass the cottage door :
Are they six ? she counts them seven—
  Are they seven ? she counts one more.

When the sun swings high in the heavens,
  And the reapers go shouting home,
She calls to the household, saying
  "Make haste! for the binders have come!
And Johnnie will want his dinner—
  He was always a hungry child;"
And they answer " Yes, it is waiting ;"
  Then tell you "her brain is wild."

Again, in the hush of the evening,
  When the work of the day is done,
And the binders go singing homeward
  In the last red rays of the sun,
She will sit at the threshold waiting,
  And her withered face lights with joy :
"Come, Johnnie," she says, as they pass her,
  "Come in to the house, my boy."

Five summers ago, her Johnnie
  Went out in the smile o' the morn,
Singing across the meadow,
  Striding down through the corn :
He towered above the binders
  Walking on either side,
And the mother's heart within her
  Swelled with exultant pride.

For he was the light of the household ;
  His brown eyes were wells of truth,

And his face was the face of the morning,
   Lit with its pure, fresh youth ;
And his song rang out from the hill-tops,
   Like the mellow bl st of a horn.
As he strode o'er the fresh shorn meadows,
   And down through the rows of corn.

But hushed were the voices of singing,
   Hushed by the presence of death,
As back to the cottage they bore him—
   In the noontide's scorching breath.
For the heat of the sun had slain him,
   Had smitten the heart in his breast,
And he who had towered above them
   Lay lower than all the rest.

The grain grows ripe in the sunshine,
   And the summers ebb and flow,
And the binders stride to their labor,
   And sing as they come and go ;
But never again from the hill-tops
   Echoes the voice like a horn ;
Never up from the meadows,
   Never back from the corn.

Yet the poor, crazed brain of the mother
   Fancies him always near ;
She is blest in her strange delusion,

For she knoweth no pain, no fear :
And always she counts the binders
   As they pass her cottage door ;
Are they six, she counts them seven :
   Are they seven, she counts one more.

1870.

TRUST.

Once Pain beat on my heart,
   And well-nigh killed it.
I shuddered at the smart,
   But said " God willed it."
And down and down again,
   With awful power,
Fell the great hand of Pain,
   Hour after hour.

While, like a mighty flail,
   The fierce blows hurt me,
I cried " God doth prevail :
   He'll not desert me."
Blow upon cruel blow,
   The great hand gave me,
Yet I cried " He doth know,
   And he will save me."

I did not loudly cry,
   And ask God's reason ;
I knew He'd tell me why,
   In his own season.
" In His good time," I said,
   In trusting blindness,
And I was not afraid
   To wait his kindness.

I did not trust in vain.
   God drew me nearer,
And whispered " Smile again !
   The way is clearer."
And lo ! my mortal sight
   Could reach to heaven,
My faith dispelled the night,
   And light was given.

THE COMMON LINK.

When on the crowded thoroughfare,
   Amidst the motley throng I stray,
In all the stranger faces there,
   I meet and pass from day to day,
Whether the face be young, or old,
Or wreathed in smiles, or calm, or cold,

On every brow I trace some line
That links the strangers' heart to mine.

Though a proud beauty rustles by,
   With haughty mien, I smile and say,
" You have a heart-ache—so have I :
   We both are hiding it to-day.
Though you are rich, I am poor,
We both have entered sorrow's door ;
Grief comes alike to you and me,
So we are of one family."

The richest nabob that I meet,
   The poorest delver that I see,
Youth and old age upon the street,
   Are one and all the same to me.
No heart that beats, but has its grief ;
Nor wealth, nor youth, gives full relief ;
And through the tears that sometimes fall
I claim relationship to all.

So poor, and rich, and high, and low,
   I meet upon this common plain.
Though far and wide our paths may lie,
   We entertain the same guest—Pain.
The subtle threads of this strange cord,
Draw me to mankind, and the Lord,
And through the sorrows heaven sends,
I hold all men to be my friends.

1869.

BURIED TO-DAY.

Cold is the wind, that blows up from the river.
   Cold is the blast that sweeps over the plain.
In the bleak breath of the morning I shiver—
   Shiver and weep, in my desolate pain.
She was so fair—like the beautiful lily—
   Fair, oh too fair to be hidden away.
And the grave is so dark, and so damp, and so chilly,
   And she—oh my love !—will be buried to-day.

White is the snow that is heaped on the meadow,
   Whiter the face, in this desolate room.
Low in the valley lurk darkness and shadow—
   Low lies my heart, in its sorrow and gloom.
How the spades scrape, on the sods they are breaking,
   Breaking, and cutting the snowdrifts away.
How the men bend to the grave they are making,
   Where she—oh my love !—will be buried to-day.

Thick are the walls ! but the bleak wind will enter,
   And chill her through all her long slumber, I know.
Rich are her robes ! but the merciless Winter
   Will beat on her breast, with its tempests of snow.
Oh she was guarded, and shielded from sorrow—
   Kept from the shadows. and darkness, alway.
But she will lie, as the beggar to-morrow—
   My love—oh my love !—that is buried to-day.

                                   1870.

WHEN I DIE.

Often, when I am alone,
   Thinking of the " things unseen ;"
Things to our eyes never shown,
   Hidden by the veil between
This world and eternity—
   To be lifted by and by,
Oft the thought has come to me,
   " Who will robe me, when I die."

When the night-time swiftly nears,
   And my last sleep comes apace,
And the mourners' bitter tears
   Fall above my dying face ;
When I pass out, white and still,
   Where no mortal hand can save,
Out beyond the reach of skill—
   Who will robe me, for the grave ?

When my work is all complete,
   And I have no more to do,
And I pass with willing feet,
   From the old life, to the new ;
While my dear ones numb with woe,
   Weep above my pulseless heart,
Who, of all the friends I know,
   Who will robe me to depart ?

Who will fold my pallid hands,
   On my quiet bosom ; close
Eyes that gaze on other lands,
   Clothe me for my last repose ?
When soft fingers toy and play
   With my tresses tenderly,
Oft the thought has come to me,
   " Will *these* robe me, when I die ?"

———

THE UNSEEN THORN.

" Cinnamon Roses !" she said, " how fair,"
   Holding them out in her finger-tips.
" Yes," I whispered, " the hue they wear
   Was borrowed out of thy cheeks, and lips.
Beautiful roses ! and each supposes
   Itself replete, with thy graces, Sweet.
Fair they may be, yet not like thee—
   See ! they fade at thy smile, dear maid !"

" Give me a Rose !" and nothing loth,
   She tossed a beautiful bud to me.
But I gathered the maid and the flowers both—
   Close to my breast.   " Not that, but *thee !*
I most am wanting.   The dear face haunting
   My heart each hour, is the sweetest flower."

And I gathered close the face like a rose,
   And kissed her lips and her finger-tips.

The leaves, from the roses in her hand,
   Dropped one by one : but the *thorn* was left.
(Fool, that I did not understand.)
   Cheated, and jilted, and all bereft,
Of the fair, false blossom I held on my bosom
   I stand to-day.   But the *thorn* alway
Pierces my heart like a cruel dart.
   The rose is dead : and her love—has fled.

                    1870.

FATHER AND CHILD.

Th New Year wedded the winter—
   Winter, the harsh old king !
Whose head was a snow-capped mountain—
   Whose breath was the North-Wind's sting.
But he wooed and wedded the maiden,
   And gave her a robe of snow ;
And hung on her breast bright jewels,
   With a lace-work of frost below.

And the days flowed on like a river ;
   And the mother looked up and smiled,
When she laid in the arms of Winter,

Their beautiful first-born child.
And what shall we name our infant?"
  She said to the harsh old king.
And the old man kissed her softly,
  And said, " we will call her Spring."

"And how shall we robe our darling?
  I have always dressed in white !
But she must be clothed in colors—
  With something soft, and bright."
And the old man smiled and answered,
  " We will give her a robe of green ;
Trimmed with the fairest flowers,
  And buds, that were ever seen !"

And he kissed the beautiful infant,
  Softly on cheek, and brow,
And he clasped the hand of the mother,
  And said " I am going now !
The days of my life were numbered,
  And the last is slipping away.
But I leave you to guard our darling,
  Wherever her steps shall stray."

1870.

———

UNDER THE MOON.

Under the moon two lovers walked— ·
  The silver moon—the round, full moon ;

Under its beams they softly talked,
   Of youth, and love, and June.
And they plighted their vows in the silvery light,
For their hearts, like the moon, were full, that night.

Under the moon they walked again—
   The setting the moon—the waning moon.
And scarcely a word was said by the twain.
   (Ah moon, you set too soon.)
For love, in one o' the hearts, like the rim
Of the waning moon, grew faint, and dim.

Under the skies a maiden stood—
   The cold night skies—the moonless skies :
She heard the owl in the lonely wood,
   And she heard her own deep sighs.
"Heart and skies devoid of light ;
Oh God !" she cried, "what a dreary night !"

Under the skies is a narrow mound—
   The watchful skies—the starry skies.
And the rays of the moon, so full and round,
   Shine down, where the maiden lies.
And they shine on the fickle lover, who
Walks with another, and woos anew.

SINGERS.

The sweetest songs that were ever sung,
  And those that please the best,
Though sorrow, and grief, and tears were wrung
  From some o'er-burdened breast.
Through the words breathe only of mirth, and bloom,
  And the strains are the gladdest and lightest,
Remember that after a night of gloom,
  The rays of the sun are brightest.

The rain must fall, ere the spring-time grass
  Grows tender, and green, and sweet.
Through the pangs of travail a soul must pass,
  Ere a song is born complete.
After a winter of storm, and snow,
  Blossom the buds in our bowers :
After a season of tears and woe,
  Blossom the poet's flowers.

There are few who give the poet a thought,
  When they read the pleasing strain.
There are few who know that a poem is wrought
  Through sorrow, and tears, and pain.
The merriest song, and the blithest lay,
  And those that are sweetest and gladdest,
Are woven in gloomy and cheerless days,
  When the poet's heart is the saddest.

TAKE MY HAND.

I am walking in the darkness :
   All around me is the night.
I am groping in the shadows,
   And I cannot see the light.
Every sunbeam has departed ;
   There is gloom throughout the land.
I am fainting by the wayside—
   Heavenly Father, take my hand.

Oh, the paths are rough and thorny,
   That my weary feet have trod.
I am bleeding—I am dying,
   Take me by the hand, O God !
Let my gloomy way be lighted,
   By the glory of Thy face !
And thy broad and mighty bosom,
   Let it be my resting place.

Through this awful night of sorrow,
   Father, let me hear thy voice.
Teach me how to sing in anguish—
   How to suffer, and rejoice.
Take me by the hand, and guide me,
   Lead me in the better way.
Through this vale of storm, and tempest,
   To the land of perfect day.

Strengthen me for every contest :
　　Let my prayer be not in vain.
I would bless thee in my sorrow—
　　I would glory in my pain.
Make my spirit white, for heaven !
　　Let my soul be purified
In the blood that flowed so freely,
　　From the wound in Jesus' side.

Gird my soul, oh God, for battle !
　　I am weak, O make me strong.
Do not let my courage falter,
　　Though the strife be fierce, and long.
And upon Thy hand, my Father,
　　Let me keep a clinging hold,
Till I cross the pearly portal,
　　To the city built of gold.

　　　　　　　　　　　　　　1869.

———

DISINTERRED.

[Written after the attempt of Sensation Lovers to prove that
Shakespeare's plays were written by Lord Bacon.]

Lo ! here's another corpse exhumed !
　　Another Poet disinterred !
Sensation cried, " Dig up the grave,
　　And let the dust be hoed and stirred ;
Ayd bring the bones of Shakespeare out !
'Twill edify the throng, no doubt.

" The Byron scandal has grown old !
    That rare tit-bit is flat, and stale.
The throng is gaping for more food !
    We need a new sensation tale.
Old Shakespeare sleeps too well, and sound.
Tear off the shroud—dig up the ground !

" We have exhumed poor ' Raven Poe,'
    And proved beyond the shade of doubt,
He saw no raven, after all.
    Now trot the bones of Shakespeare out !
Byron, and Poe, and Shakespeare—good !
Who shall we serve up next for food ?"

And who, say I, oh seers of earth !
    What corpse comes next ? I daily look
To see if some sage hasn't proved
    That Jones, or Smith, wrote Lalla Rook !
Or Blifkins lent his brains to Moore—
Who was a plagairst, and boor.

Sensation, keep your servants out ;
    Let them be watchful, and alert !
We'll need a new discovery soon :
    Tell them to dig about the dirt,
And tear off Keats', or Shelly's shroud,
To please and edify the crowd.

1870.

A LAWYER'S ROMANCE.

Into the mellow light of the cloudless autumn day,
Somehow, the vision slips, of a landscape, far away,
Wherever I turn my eyes, it hovers before them still,
The little, vine-wreathed cot, on the southerly slope of the
　　hill,

The pasture at the left, the ducks a-swim in the pond,
And the straight, green rows of corn, with the wheat fields
　　just beyond,
The sloping lawn on the right, that is always seeming to
　　say
To the lake that lies below, " I will meet you just half
　　way."

And over and over the cot, from th' ground to th' mossy
　　eaves,
Cling, and twine. and clamber the vines, with their dark,
　　green leaves ;
The little mimic garden, with its simple flowers a-blow,
Larkspur, bleeding hearts, and the clumps of phlox, like
　　snow ;

Petunias, red and white, like drooping and fragile maids,
Rose trees hanging down, with roses of many shades,
Marigolds, batchelor-buttons, with clusters of evergreen,
On the two trim rows of beds, with the narrow path
　　between,

And the setting rays of the sun, lending it all a flush,
That is given to sunset scenes, by the heavenly Artist's
    brush.
It is thus it rises to-day, and hovers before my eyes ;
I have seen it softly lit, with the mornings' sweet surprise—

I have seen it when the dew glistened upon the grass—
In the hush of the summer noon, when the calm lake lay
    like glass—
In the ghostly rays o' the moon—in the quiet of the
    night—
But never half so fair as under that sunset light.

Ah ! foolish, and weak old heart, must you live it over
    again ?
Why reopen the book, whose final page was Pain !
But the picture rises before me, rises, and hovers there,
And the glory of the sunset falls on the maiden's hair ;

The maid, who stood in that garden ten long summers
    ago,
Stood by the "bleeding hearts," and the clusters of phlox,
    like snow.
Ah ! musty and dusty old heart, you were younger and
    lighter then !
Yet not young, for now you have beat, two score years
    and ten ;

But that one summer holds the essence of all my life,
The forty years before were records of toil and strife,

And I opened the book again, when my holiday was o'er,
And began at the page I left, and plodded on as before.

Weary of law, of work, of the dust, and heat of th' town,
Ill, in body and mind, my heart went longing down
To the cool, green country meadows ; and I followed it
  one day,
And there in the vine-wreathed cot, let the summer slip
  away ;

Ay ! and I let the heart I had guarded forty years—
The heart that had never been stirred by love's wild
  hopes and fears—
I let it slip away to the maid with amber eyes,
With tresses dusky brown, and cheeks like th' sunset
  skies·

Ah ! secret I tried to keep, ah ! love I strove to hide !
But in the July twilight, I lingered at her side,
And, leaning by the rose tree, her tresses swept my
  cheek !
"Ah ! sweet," I cried in a tremor, "I love you—let me
  speak !"

And then, somehow the love I had thought to guard
  untold
Broke loose from the fetters of silence, and gathered
  strength, and rolled

Forth in a torrent of words ; and I knelt at the maiden's
    feet,
Crying, " Grant me a token, as yea or nay, my sweet."

And then, with a shy, sweet smile, she gave me her
    finger-tips,
And, bolder grown, I said, as I raised them to my lips,
" 'Twere a lesser love than mine, that were wholly
    satisfied,
With a touch of your finger tips, and farther than that
    denied."

The curtains of her eyes dropped low, and I drew her
    close,
And over and over again kissed the sweet face like a
    rose.
I said, " I have pleaded a case, and won it ; do you see ?
And now I take my pay ! for a lawyer must have his fee."

Ah ! summer over and gone, into the echoless past !
Oh ! August afternoons, that drifted by too fast !
Oh ! rows on the quiet lake, in the blissful moonlit eves,
When the harvesters sang their song, carrying home the
    sheaves.

I can hear it even now, the voices, strong ond sweet,
Over the noise, and rattle, and roar of the busy street,

I can see the face of Mable, full lipped, ripe, and fair,
With the amber tints in her eyes, and the dusky shades
　　on her hair.

Into my life's September, came the beauty I missed in
　　June,
The glory lost in the morning, came in the afternoon.
The dream that belongs to youth, golden—complete—
　　sublime,
I dreamed not, in the spring, but in the autumn time.

Ah! and the young heart wakes from the dream of love,
　　and then,
Suffers a little while, and dreams it over again.
But never a second draught of the wine of love for me,
I drank it all at the first, and shattered the cup, you see.

I woke from the golden dream when I saw *her* on the
　　breast
Of a fair-faced, beardless youth—when I saw his red lips
　　pressed
Over and over again to the mouth, like a rose half blown,
And I heard her whispered words—" My only love, my
　　own."

Hush! censure them not! His heart she toyed with
　　even as mine.
He suffered keenly, I think, then knelt at another's
　　shrine.

And she—speak softly of her—she died: she is only dust;
Died repentant—forgiven—and entered Heaven—I trust.

And I—well my years drift on, as my two-score drifted
    away,
Only at times, this memory comes, as it came to-day,
Thrilling me through and through—and I live it all once
    more,
Though I shut the past away, and have striven to lock
    the door.

Have I lost all faith in woman?   Nay, surely not: should
    we
Say that every heart is false because *one* proves to be !
Because I find a worm in the petals of a rose,
Shall I say that worms are coiled in every flower that
    blows ?

Nay, there are constant woman, and women as sweet and
    fair
As she with the amber eyes, and the shadows on her hair.
But I found the wine of love so late, that when I quaffed
I held none in reserve, but drank it all at a draught.

The future? I do not dread: it is neither dark nor bright.
I have had my day of joy—I have had my sorrow's night.
God helped me through the last—I do not know just
    how,
    12

But He answered when I called Him, and why should I
   doubt him now?

Nor mortal eye can see, nor mortal heart conceive,
What He holdeth in His kingdom for the faithful that
   believe.
But I sometimes think the dream that was broken here
   for me,
I shall finish and complete by the shining Jasper sea.

· 1870.

A SUMMER DAY.

There's a gaping rent in the curtain
   That longs for a needle and thread,
There's a garment that ought to be finished,
   And a book that wants to be read.
There's a letter that needs to be answered,
   There are clothes to fold away,
And I know these tasks are waiting,
   And ought to be done to-day.

But how can I mend the curtain,
   While watching this silvery cloud,
And how can I finish th' garment,
   When the robin calls so loud.
And the whispering trees are telling

Such stories above my head,
That I can but lie and listen,
   And the book is all unread.

If I try to write the letter,
   I am sure one half the words
Will be in the curious language
   Of my chattering friends, the birds.
The lilacs bloom in the sunshine,
   The roses nod and smile,
And the clothes that ought to be folded
   And ironed, must wait awhile.

I lie in the locust shadows,
   And gaze at the summer sky,
Bidding the cares and toubles
   And trials of life pass by.
The beautiful locust blossoms
   Are falling about my feet,
And the dreamy air is laden
   With their odors rare and sweet.

The honey-bees hum in the clover,
   The grasses rise and fall,
The robin stops and listens,
   As he hears the brown thrush call.
The humming-bird sings to me softly,
   The butterfly flits away—

Oh what could be sweeter than living,
This beautiful summer day !

1869.

———

SONG AND MAID.

A poet toiled over a song, for the maid
   Who had plighted her troth to him.
And he leaned, and wrote, in the gathering shade,
   Till his eyes were dim.

But the maiden strolled on the distant beach,
And listed another's tender speech.

The poet sang of her love-lit eye,
   So softly, and deeply blue ;
How its soulful glance—half arch, half shy,
   He only knew.

But the maid's blue eyes were shedding their light
On the face of a tall, dark man, that night.

He sang of her hand, so white, and fair,
   And soft as a hand could be.
"And the ring," he sang, " that is gleaming there
   Binds her to me,"

But the maid to her tall companion said,
"This ring? ' tis the gift of a friend, now dead."

He sang of her ripe and dewy lips—
  "They are roses before they blow.
And the taste of the nectar that from them drips
  I only know."

But the maid, as she walked in the moonlight mist,
Lifted her face, and was lovingly kissed.

He sang of her voice, "It is soft and clear
  As the voice of a gentle dove.
So tender, that I alone can hear
  Her words of love."

But the maiden whispered to one by the sea,
"I love thee, darling, and only thee."

Ah, poet! finish your last light strain :
  Ah, maid! shall we give you praise, or blame?
You are wringing a heart, with bitter pain,
  Yet helping to laurel a brow with fame.

For out of the depths of a master woe,
  And through the valley of dark despair,
The soul of a singer must grope, and go,
  Ere he wear the purple true poets wear.

ASLEEP.

"Come closer," she said, "my sister,
　For I can not see your face.
The day grows dim, and the shadows grim,
　Are gathering on apace.
I am glad that the night is coming :
　I am weary, and want to rest.
What ! do you weep, that I fall asleep
　Leaning upon your breast ?

"Oh, Sister, I am *so* tired :
　How tired you can not know.
And a jarring pain, in my weary brain,
　Beats like a cruel blow.
I think it will all have vanished,
　After I sleep awhile.
How sweetly I rest, lying here on your breast.
　In the warmth of your loving smile.

"Such a beautiful dream, my sister,
　I dreamed while I slept last night.
I thought he was true : and he came with you,
　And kissed me in love's delight.
And he said——　But I am so weary,
　I will sleep ere I tell the rest."
But the sister wept, for the maiden slept
　In the sleep of death, on her breast.

1869.

TWO COUNTS.

If I count my life by the ticking of clocks,
  In the old methŏdical way,
If I count by the years, and the years' twelve blocks,
If I figure it out by the ceaseless flocks
  Of hours that make a day,
If I count from the annual calendar,
And trust to the measured years in there,
  Well, then I have turned, we'll say,
But a notch, or two, on the wheel of time ;
I am still in the flush of my youths' glad prime ;
        My life is new,
          As the count will say.
        I am scarcelythrough
          With the opening play.
        I am, in truth,
          In the flush of youth,
If I trust to ticking and striking of clocks,
And count by the years, and the years' twelve blocks.

If I count my life by the beat, throb, beat,
  Of the weary heart in my breast,
If I count by the aims that have met defeat,
  And the vain, vain search for rest,
        If I count by tears,
          And by haunting fears,
      By hopes that were all in vain,

By dear trusts shattered,
　　And good ships battered,
And lost on the treacherous main,
　　By faith unfounded,
　　And love death-wounded,
If I reckon it thus, why then
Counting this way, I have lived, we'll say,
　　Full three-score years, and ten.

1870.

THE WATCHER.

" I think I hear the sound of horses' feet,
　　Beating upon the gravelled avenue.
Go to the window that looks on the street !
　　He would not let me die, alone, I knew !"
Back to the couch the patient watcher passed,
And said, " It is the wailing of the blast."

She turned upon her couch, and seeming, slept,
　　The long, dark lashes, shadowing her cheek.
And on, and on, the weary moments crept,
　　When suddenly the watcher heard her speak,
" I think I hear the sound of horses' hoofs !"
And answered, " 'Tis the rain, upon the roofs."

Unbroken silence : quiet, deep, profound.
　　The restless sleeper turns. " How dark ! how late !

What is it that I hear—that trampling sound ?
  I think there is a horseman at the gate !"
The watcher turns away her eyes, tear-blind.
" It is the shutter, beating in the wind."

The dread night passed. The patient clock ticked on.
  The weary watcher moved not from her place.
The gray, dun shadows of the early dawn,
  Caught sudden glory, from the sleeper's face.
"He comes! my love! I knew he would!" she cried,
  And, smiling sweetly in her slumbers, died.

1870.

LIFE AND DEATH.

Three days agone, and she was here:
  Her light step on the stair was springing.
Her sweet voice fell upon my ear ;
  (She mocked the thrushes in her singing.)
The billows of her long, bright hair
  Fell round her, in a golden splendor.
Her face was young and fresh and fair ;
  Her eyes were innocent and tender.

Her presence filled the house : each room
  Breathed of her pure and sweet existence.
She was like some rare plant in bloom,

Its fragrance reaching through the distance.
Here was her ribbon—there her book,
  Beyond, her wreath, or faded flower.
A step, a voice, a laugh, a look,
  Told of her presence, hour by hour.

How strange is life !" I said, " From naught
  God fashioned out this glowing creature.
Endowed with motion, feeling thought—
  Perfect in symmetry, and feature.
Sweeter than any opening rose,
  All grace and beauty hangs about her.
Though every flower were left that blows,
  Earth would be bare and bleak, without her."

Three days agone ! ay ! life is strange,
  But death is stranger, vaster, deeper.
It brings us tears, and gloom, and change.
  She was God's sheaf, and Death His reaper.
Three days ! and now no voice is heard—
  No light step on the stair is bounding.
In vain the tuneful-throated bird
  Listens to hear her answer sounding.

I cannot find her, anywhere !
  How vast and strange the mystic power,
That leaves but one soft strand of hair,
  Of all that golden, shining shower.

In door, and out, in every place,
   I search and seek ; oh, vain endeavor !
The voice, the laugh, the form, the face,
   Have vanished from the earth forever.

A spot of ground, a fresh-turned sod,
   Hides what was beautiful and mortal.
Her spirit (fairer still) to God,
   And life eternal, crossed the portal.
Frailer than any opening rose,
   The winds of earth blew cold about her.
Fairer than any flower that grows,
   Heaven was not complete without her.

                  1872.

AN AUTUMN REVERIE.

Through all the weary, hot midsummer time,
   My heart has struggled with its awful grief.
And I have waited for these autumn days,
   Thinking the cooling winds would bring relief.
For I remembered how I loved them once,
   When all my life was full of melody.
And I have looked and longed for their return,
   Nor thought but they would seem the same, to me.

The fiery summer burned itself away,
   And from the hills, the golden autumn time

Looks down and smiles. The fields are tinged with
    brown—
  The birds are talking of another clime.
The forest trees are dyed in gorgeous hues,
  And weary ones have sought an earthy tomb.
But still the pain tugs fiercely at my heart—
  And still my life is wrapped in awful gloom.

The winds I thought would cool my fevered brow,
  Are bleak, and dreary ; and they bear no balm.
The sounds I thought would soothe my throbbing brain,
  Are grating discords ; and they can not calm
This inward tempest. Still it rages on.
  My soul is tost upon a troubled sea,
I find no pleasure in the olden joys—
  The autumn is not as it used to be.

I hear the children shouting at their play !
  Their hearts are happy, and they know not pain.
To them the day brings sunlight, and no shade.
  And yet I would not be a child again.
For surely as the night succeeds the day,
  So surely will their mirth turn into tears.
And I would not return to happy hours,
  If I must live again these weary years.

I would walk on, and leave it all behind :
  will walk on ; and when my feet grow sore,

The boatman waits—his sails are all unfurled—
    He waits to row me to a fairer shore.
My tired limbs shall rest on beds of down,
    My tears shall all be wiped by Jesus' hand ;
My soul shall know the peace it long hath sought—
    A peace too wonderful to understand.

1868.

TWO LIVES.

An infant lies in her cradle bed :
    The hands of sleep, on her eyelids fall.
The moments pass, with a noiseless tread,
    And the clock on the mantle counts them all.
The infant wakes, with a wailing cry,
But she does not heed, how her life slips by.

A child is sporting, in careless play :
    She rivals the birds with her mellow song :
The clock, unheeded, ticks away,
    And counts the moments that drift along.
But the child is chasing the butterfly,
And she does not heed how her life drifts by.

A maiden stands at her lover's side,
    In the tender light of the setting sun.

Onward and onward the moments glide,
   And the old clock counts them, one by one.
But the maiden's bridal is drawing nigh,
And she does not heed how her life drifts by.

A song of her youth the matron sings,
   And she dreameth a dream, and her eye is wet.
And backward and forward the pendlum swings,
   In the clock that never has rested yet.
And the matron smothers a half-drawn sigh,
As she thinks how her life is drifting by.

An old crone sits in her easy chair ;
   Her head is dropped on her aged breast.
The clock on the mantle ticketh there—
   The clock that is longing now for rest.
And the old crone smiles, as the moments fly,
   And thinks how her life is drifting by.

A shrouded form, in a coffin bed -
   A waiting grave, in the fallow ground :
The moments pass with a noiseless tread,
   But the clock on the mantle makes no sound.
The lives of the two have gone for ay,
And they do not heed, how the time drifts by.

                              1869.

IN MEMORIUM.

(Miss Jennie Blanchard, age'd 21)

Across the sodden field we gaze,
   To woodlands, painted gold and brown ;
To hills that hide in purple haze,
   And proudly wear the autumn's crown.
Oh, lavish autumn ! fair, we know,
And yet we cannot deem her so.

The blossoms had their little day ;
   The grasses, and the green-hung trees.
They lived, grew old, and passed away.
   And yet, not satisfied with these,
The cruel autumn could not pass
Without this last fell stroke : alas !

" Alas," we cry, because God's ways
   Seem so at variance with our own,
And grieving through the nights and days,
   We see not that His love was shown
In gathering to the " Harvest Home,"
Our lost one, from the grief to come.

Oh, Tears ! she will not have to weep !
   Oh, Woes ! she will not have to bear !
For her, who fell so soon asleep,

No furrowed face, no whitened hair.
And yet *we* would have given her *these*,
In lieu of heavenly victories.

How weak the strongest mortal love !
  How selfish in its tenderness !
How God's angelic host above
  Must wonder at our blind distress !
We see her still grave, dark and dim,
And *they* see only Heaven and *Him.*

Perpetual youth ! oh, priceless boon !
  For ever youthful : never old !
How can we think she died too soon ?
  What though life's story *was* half told ?
Wiser than all earth's seers, to-day,
Is this fair soul, that passed away.

Magician, sage, philosopher,
  With all their vast brain-wealth combined,
Are only babes, compared with her :
  This soul, that left the " things behind,"
And, " reaching to the things before,"
Gained God, through Christ, forevermore.

October, 1870.

MY LOVE.

My love is fair as the morn ;
  Yes, fair as the summer morning,
When with fold on fold of red, and gold,
  The sun in the east gives warning,
And a soft, rare light, not dim nor bright,
  O'er hill and mountain lingers ;
And flower, and vine with jewels shine—
  Bedecked by the fairie's fingers.

My love has eyes like the clouds,
  That are dyed with the autumn's splendor,
So darkly blue, where her soul looks through—
  So truthful and so tender.
When their light is hid by the snowy lid,
  My heart seems lost in shadow.
And her glance will chase the gloom from my face,
  Like sunlight on a meadow.

My love has cheeks like a rose—
  Yes, like a rose in blossom,
And a flake of snow is her polished brow,
  And a drift of snow is her bosom ;
And her hair sweeps down, half gold, half brown,
  Like a silken veil, to cover
The matchless grace of her form and face,
  From the burning eyes of her lover.

13

My love has a voice like a thrush—
 Yes, like a thrush when singing.
And the wondering lark cries, " Listen ! hark !"
 When he hears her glad tone ringing.
Oh she is fair, beyond compare ;
 And how her sweet face flushes,
When I whisper low a tale we know—
 And the rose is shamed by her blushes.

1871.

THE FROST FAIRY.

All day the trees were moaning,
 For the leaves that they had lost.
All day they creaked, and trembled,
 And the naked branches tossed,
And shivered in the north wind,
 As he hurried up and down,
Over hill tops, bleak and cheerless,
 Over meadows, bare, and brown.

"Oh, my green and tender leaflets !
 Oh, my fair buds, lost, and gone !"
So they moaned through all the day-time,
 So they groaned, till night came on.
And the hoar-frost lurked, and listened,
 To the wailing, sad refrain.

And he whispered, " Wait, be patient ;
  I will cover you again.

" I will clothe you in new garments :
  I will deck you, ere the light,
In a sheen of spotless glory,
  In a robe of purest white.
You shall wear the matchless mantle
  That the good frost-fairy weaves."
And the bare trees listened, wondered—
  And forgot their fallen leaves.

And the quaint and silent fairy,
  Backward, forward, through the gloom,
Wove the matchless, glittering mantle ;
  Spun the frost-thread, on her loom.
And the bare trees talked together—
  Talked in whispers, soft, and low,
While the good and patient fairy
  Moved her shuttle to and fro.

And, lo ! when the sudden glory
  Of the morning crept abroad,
All the trees were clothed in grandeur ;
  All the twiglets robed and shod
In the glittering, spotless garments,
  That the sunshine decked with gems ;
And the trees forgot their sorrow,
  Neath their robes and diadems.

1870.

THE SUMMONS.

I think the leaf would sooner
   Be the first to break away,
Than to hang alone in the orchard
   In the bleak November day.
And I think the fate of the flower
   That falls in the midst of bloom
Is sweeter than if it lingered
   To die in the autumn's gloom.

Some glowing, golden morning
   In the heart of the summer time,
As I stand in the perfect vigor
   And strength of my youth's glad prime;
When my heart is light and happy,
   And the world seems bright to me,
I would like to drop from this earth-life,
   As a green leaf drops from the tree.

Some day, when the golden glory
   Of June is over the earth,
And the birds are singing together
   In a wild, mad strain of mirth,
When the skies are as clear and cloudless
   As the skies of June can be,
I would like to have the summons
   Sent down from God to me.

I would not wait for the furrows—
  For the faded eyes and hair;
But pass out swift and sudden,
  Ere I grow heart-sick with care;
I would break some morn in my singing—
  Or fall in my springing walk,
As a full-blown flower will sometimes
  Drop, all a-bloom, from the stalk.

And so, in my youth's glad morning,
  While the summer walks abroad,
I would like to hear the summons,
  That must come, sometime, from God.
I would pass from the earth's perfection
  To the endless June above;
From the fullness of living and loving,
  To the noon of Immortal Love.

                              1873.

THREE YEARS OLD.

Written upon Eva Orton's third birthday.

A robbin up in the linden-tree
  Merrily sings this lay:
"Somebody sweet is three years old—

Three years old to-day."
Somebody's bright blue eyes look up
    Through tangled curls of gold,
And two red lips unclose to say—
    "To-day I am free years old."

Clouds were over the sky this morn,
    But now they are sailing away;
Clouds could never obscure the sun
    On somebody sweet's birthday.
Bluest of skies and greenest of trees,
    Sunlight and birds and flowers,
These are Nature's birthday gifts
    To this sweet pet of ours.

The pantry is brimming with cakes and creams
    For somebody's birthday ball.
Papa and mamma bring their gifts,
    But their *love* is better than all.
Ribbons and sashes, and dainty robes,
    Gifts of silver and gold,
Will fade and rust as the days go by,
    But their *hearts* will not grow cold.

Then laugh in the sunlight, somebody sweet—
    Little flower of June!
You have nothing to do with care,
    For life is in perfect tune.

Loving hearts and sheltering arms
   Shall keep old care away
For many a year, from somebody sweet,
   Who is three years old to-day.

MILWAUKEE, June 26, '73.

THE DIFFERENCE.

Up in the cosy chamber,
   Where, on the snowy bed
The dress, and the pearls, and the new false curls,
   For the morrow's use were spread,
The bride elect and her mother
   Were sitting before the grate,
Talking over the days gone by,
   And planning the future state.

"I really am quite well suited,"
   Said Minnie, "with my outfit—
Jane says Kit Somers trousseau,
   Is nothing compared with it.
That her laces are imitation,
   And her bonnet a perfect fright,
And she says I'll wholly eclipse her
   In everybody's sight.

"And she isn't to make the tour,
    But only to visit awhile.
I declare I'd never be married
    If I couldn't do it in style.
Jane says her jewels, though splendid,
    With mine can never compare:
I tell you I do love Harry,
    When I look at this solitaire.

"And I think he's a darling, mother,
    For he's going to let me board,
At least he will, he says, until
    He finds that he can afford
To purchase that house of Mosleys,
    That splendid brown stone front.
I wouldn't have anything humbler,
    And Harry says *he* wont.

"My presents are perfectly splendid,
    Much finer than Kit's, I know,
I think that's half of a wedding
    To have such things to show.
If we get that house of Mosleys,
    What a brilliant life we'll live.
Such people as I'll have throng it—
    Such parties as I will give.

I mean to just *queen it* mother,
    In society everywhere,

And my title of belle of the City
  I shall continue to wear.
I dont believe that a woman
  By marriage should be tied down
To wearing a smile for her husband
  And for all other men a frown.

"I mean to dress better than ever,
  And be just as merry and free.
Children! the troublesome wretches!
  No ma'm, not any for me.
I know I'd be cross and unhappy,
  With children to tease, and annoy.
A joy, you say, to be mother,
  Well, I will be spared that joy."

Across the hall in their bedroom
  A hale old couple sat,
Minnies' grandfather and mother,
  Having a good night chat.
"So the last of the children is going,"
  Grandmother said, and sighed,
"Minnie, (we named her Mary,)
  To-morrow will be a bride.

"It will be a great occasion,
  All glitter and glow and shine,
A nineteenth century wedding,

Not much like yours, and mine.
A few good friends were with us,
　　When we were married, John,
They came to see us united—
　　Not to see what the bride had on.

"I wore a snowy muslin,
　　And a white rose in my hair,
No silks nor gems, nor diadems—
　　And yet you thought me fair.
We stood in the broad cool kitchen,
　　On the white and sanded floor,
And a breeze from the odorous orchard,
　　Looked in at the open door.

"The minister read the service
　　That made us one for life,
And I was no longer a maiden
　　But a loved and cherished wife.
You took me home on the morrow!
　　Six miles, in a one horse chaise;
Folks didn't race over the country
　　'Touring' in these old days.

"Our house was a tiny cabin
　　That would just hold two, you said,
But ere a year, you found, my dear
　　There was room for three, instead.

Ah me! that wonderful baby!
  'Twas a moment of perfect bliss
When I held up the pink faced darling
  For his father's tender kiss.

" Then came a dear little daughter!
  And then more boys and girls
Till you built on a wing to the cabin
  To cover their sunny curls.
There was never a happier woman
  In all of the land I know,
Singing away at my labor—
  Watching the children grow.

" I had my beaux and lovers,
  When I was a girl ; but when
I became your bride I put aside
  All thoughts of other men.
Lover, and king, and husband,
  And friend, I found in you.
And you repaid my devotion,
  By being kind, and true.

"Ah well! the world keeps changing
  And weddings have changed with the rest,
People go only to comment
  And see how the bride is drest.
Girls wed houses and titles

Instead of men as of old,
And babies are out of the fashion
    And all that glitters is gold.

"Perhaps these times are better,
    Though I cannot think them so,
But I am a poor old woman,
    And not supposed to know."
And grandmother finished her musings
    With a meaning shake of the head
Over nineteenth century folly,
    And sighed, and went to bed.

                                    1872.

———

LOVES EXTRAVAGANCE.

Could I but measure my strength, by my love,
    Were I as strong, as my heart's love is true,
I would pull down the stars, from the heavens above,
    And weave them all into a garland for you.
And brighter, and better, your jewels should be
    Than any proud queen's, that e'r dwelt o'er the sea.
Ay! richer and rarer, your gems, love, should be
    Than any rare jewels that come from the sea.

I would gather the beautiful, delicate green
    From the dress of the spring—with the heavens soft blue,
And never from east land, to west land were seen

Such wonderful robes, as I'd fashion for you.
And I'd snatch the bright rays of the sun in my hand
  And braid you a girdle, love, strand over strand.
Ay! one by one, catch the bright rays in my hand
  And braid them, and twine them, all strand over strand.

I would gather the amber, the red and gold dyes,
  That glimmer and glow, in the autumn sunset,
And weave you a mantle; and pull from the skies
  The rainbow to trim it. Ah Love! never yet
Was any proud princess, from east to the west
  So peerlessly jeweled—so royally drest.
Never daughter of princes, in east land or west,
  So decked in rare jewels, so gorgeously drest.

And I'd make you a vail, from the rare golden haze,
  Than Indian Summer spreads over the lea.
And trim it with dew! Queens should envy and praise
  Your matchless apparel, ah darling, but see—
My strength is unequal to what I would do!
  I have only this little low cottage, for you.
Nay! I can not accomplish the thing I would do,
  And I've only this cot and a warm heart for you.

1870.

YOU WILL FORGET ME.

You will forget me the years are so tender—
  They bind up the wounds which we think are so deep;

This dream of our youth will fade out as the splendor
  Fades from the sky, when the sun sinks to sleep:
The clouds of forgetfulness, over and over,
  Will banish the last rosy colors away;
And th' fingers of Time will weave garlands to cover
  The scar which you think is a life-mark to-day.

You will forget me:—will thank me for saying
  The words which you think are so pointed with pain,
Time loves a new lay; and the dirge he is playing
  Will change for you soon to a livelier strain.
I shall pass from your life, I shall pass out forever,
  And the hours we have spent, will be sunk in the past.
Youth buries its dead: grief kills seldom, or never,
  And forgetfulness covers all sorrows at last.

You will forget me; the one thing you covet
  Now, above all things will soon seem no prize:
And the heart which is not in your keeping, to prove it
  True or untrue, will lose worth in your eyes.
The one drop to-day, which you deem only wanting
  To make life a joy, will be lost in Time's stream;
You will forget; and the ghost that is haunting
  The aisles of your heart will pass out with the dream.